Miracle at
Monty Middle School

by
Mary A. Monroe

authorHOUSE™

1663 LIBERTY DRIVE, SUITE 200
BLOOMINGTON, INDIANA 47403
(800) 839-8640
WWW.AUTHORHOUSE.COM

First published by AuthorHouse 12/06/05

ISBN: 1-4208-3970-5 (sc)

Library of Congress Control Number: 2005904319

Printed in the United States of America
Bloomington, Indiana

This book is printed on acid-free paper.

Table of Contents

Chapter 1
Journal Writing,
June 3, Last Day of School

by Marvin McDonald

Well, Mr. Martin, I doubt very much that you will actually read this entry, because I'm sure our grades are already in, but if you want some "enjoyable" summer reading, read on.

I can't believe it's the last day of my 8th grade year at Monty Middle School. Four miserable years in what should have been only 3 – grades 6, 7, 8 – except that I flunked 7th grade and had to repeat it in a D.O.P. class – Drop Out Prevention. What a loser I had for a teacher that year, Mr. Tourney. All we did was play cards, monopoly, surf the internet, eat junk food and soda, and listen to music groups on our personal CD

1

players. But we didn't complain. In fact, all of the other kids in the school were jealous of us because we didn't do any work. We all passed to the eighth grade – even spaz-Ron, who pretty much just sat in a corner by himself.

But then when I got to eighth grade, and I expected much of the same cool stuff everyday, I got the shock of my life and that was you, Mr. Martin. I had never had a black male teacher before and to say your 6 ft. 2 in. solid frame of muscle slightly intimidated my 5 ft. 2 in. 155-pound jelly shape could be an accurate statement. (Notice I used the big vocabulary word *intimidated* – just one of the things you taught me, but I don't want you to think too much of yourself, you know. And did you notice how I used the descriptive word, *jelly*?) It's hard to say if it was destiny that I took your class this year, or just fat chance. But it changed my life, 180 degrees turnaround.

But you know all about that because you made us realize that "Miracle" is not just a word, but a reality. I'll never forget that "The Power of the Pen is Mightier than the Sword." If I had to give a title to this last year of mine at good old Monty, I think I'd call it "Miracles."

Well, enjoy your summer off. As for me, I plan on doing nothing but watching TV. Oh, but I will lay off the junk food and work out. I wouldn't want to lose my 175 pounds of muscle. I may even reflect on how it all started, that very first day of school, my eighth grade, September 7.

Chapter 2
September 7, First Day of School

"Hey, McDonald, see you been eating a lot of McDonald hamburgers over the summer. You still butt-ugly, but now you fat, too!" Jesus Hernandez yelled at Marvin on the first day of 8th grade, D.O.P. (Drop Out Prevention) Class.

"Marvin not butt-ugly. You talkin' about Yo-Mama?" Markus shot back.

"Yo-Mama," said Jesus in a threatening manner, leaping up to Markus with his fists clenched.

"Yo-Mama," Markus shot back again.

"KNOCK IT OFF!" screamed Ms. Turner, "OR YOU'LL BOTH END UP SUSPENDED THE FIRST DAY OF SCHOOL!" Ms. Turner was Monty Middle

School's Title One Coordinator. She was watching our infamous 8th grade D.O.P. class because it seemed the teacher from last year had quit just last week and the principal was scrambling to find us a new teacher, which wasn't an easy task. You see, our D.O.P. class contains 12 of the most whacked-out misfit kids any teacher would NOT want to have to teach all day long. Unlike the other middle school kids who go from class to class – 6 different class periods in all – we D.O.P. kids stay in the same class all day long, from 9 a.m. to 3 p.m., and then we get one elective the last period of the day. Luckily, mine is P.E. So Ms. Turner was not thrilled at all to be here. Basically, she sat at the teacher's desk, rummaging through some notebooks she had.

Ms. Turner's cool. Most of us know her, because she works with the families that have problems – you know, like mamas that are out all night doing drugs, dads that beat their wives and kids, ugly stuff like that. Me, Marvin McDonald, well my story's not that sorry. I just have a mom who doesn't really want me right now and a dad who likes his girlfriend more than his own kid, so I usually stay over a lot at the house of my best friend – Markus.

Markus is cool. He's black, smart, and wouldn't be in D.O.P. if he didn't have such a short temper that gets him in a lot of fights. After his fifth suspension for fighting, they put him in D.O.P. last year. We hit it off right away because in some ways we're opposites, but in other ways we're just alike. Anyways, it's always better to be Markus' friend instead of his enemy!

Since Ms. Turner was pretty much ignoring us, we were all free to do whatever we wanted, which was pretty much how it was like last year. Spaz-Ron was sitting in one of the back seats, drawing pencil sketches in a white notebook, something he did for hours and hours. Quinesha and Beljania were listening to CDs on their CD players. Girthma (who insists that her new name is "Brittney") and Danielle were drawing all over the white boards and chalk boards, things like "Brittney was here," and "Danielle is hot." There was one other girl (5 in all out of our 12). She was new and looked really spooky. I guess you could say she was into "Gothic," because she had real pale white skin powder on her face and black lips. She was holding a doll's head (no body mind you), which had safety pins through its ears and skull. Like I said – spooky. She sat in the back row, three seats away from Spaz-Ron. Her name we found out was Nicole.

Of us boys, there were 7. Me, Markus, Spaz-Ron, Jesus, Roberto, Luis and Mike. Roberto, Luis and Mike were all involved in a pencil war, where each kid holds out a new pencil and you slam another pencil against it until one of the pencils break. Whoever breaks the other person's pencil wins.

It was loud, but Ms. Turner didn't seem to care. You see, they put the D.O.P. classes way in the back of the school, right next to an easy exit in case of emergency. Our school gets a lot of important people visiting all the time, and they really don't want these important people visiting us. Like I said, we were the 12 misfits of eighth grade that Monty Middle School would just like to pretty much forget about.

"HEY, KEEP IT DOWN," Ms. Turner screamed above all the noise. "I GOTTA CALL THE OFFICE AND FIND OUT IF YOUR NEW TEACHER IS HERE YET. SHUT UP!"

The class quieted down. "When do we go to lunch?" Quinesha's voice broke the silence.

"Quinesha, it's only 9:30 a.m. We're not concerned about lunch right now. Now stay quiet. I need to buzz the main office to find out where your teacher is. I have to go to a workshop at 10:00 a.m. and they said he would be here by now," Ms. Turner said.

"Bzzzzzz," Ms. Turner rang the tiny emergency button over the teacher's desk.

"Yes?" a pleasant voice answered.

"This is Ms. Turner in D.O.P. 8th. Do you know if Dr. Thornton has processed the new teacher yet? You see, I need to be in a 10:00 a.m. workshop…"

"I believe so. I think he should be there very –," the pleasant voice never had a chance to finish her sentence before the door to our class opened and in walked a huge African-American man – 6 ft. 2 in. at least – and a hush stilled the room.

"Soon."

"Thank you," said Ms. Turner. "I believe he has just arrived."

Chapter 3
Do You Believe in Miracles?

Ms. Turner made the first move. She stood up and walked toward our new teacher, extending her hand forward. After a few words were exchanged, Ms. Turner gathered up her papers and left Room 122. The momentary impact of seeing our new teacher was soon over and the 12 of us pretty much went back to what we had been doing – pencil fighting, CD listening, and loud talking. There's just something about middle school kids – we just got lots to talk about, I guess. We love to talk and play around.

"Excuse me," the new teacher said as he stood up in front of his desk.

Quinesha and Beljania became quiet and turned their attention to the teacher. I looked up. Roberto, Luis and Mike were still involved in their pencil war, and Roberto was so excited, he was jumping out of his seat and going, "Yeah, Yeah, Yeaaaah!"

"**EXCUSE ME**." His deep, baritone voice stated those two words in such a way that they demanded a response from us, which was silent attention.

"Now that's better. We are going to be a team – you and I. I am your coach and your teacher. Rule #1, when I'm standing here, it's obvious we have important work to discuss together, so that means you need to close your mouths, turn your eyes up here and pay attention."

His words rolled off his tongue like velvet; he spoke clearly, without hesitation, in a way that was both gentle and commanding. I glanced around the room. The girls – "Brittney," Danielle, Quinesha, Beljania, and Nicole – were sitting more quietly than I had ever seen them! Danielle had her hands folded in front of her, looking positively angelic! Spaz Ron was still doodling, but halfway looking up. Roberto, Luis and Mike looked more bored than anything, like they were sorry they had to stop their pencil war game. Markus looked genuinely pleased that we had a "brother" for our new teacher!

"My name is Mr. Martin. I'm a professional writer who is now entering the teaching profession."

Brittney interrupted, "How is it you be a writer?" Brittney shook her hair forward onto her right cheek, a gesture she did often. She had a large disfigured burn scar on that cheek, something she got in her native country Haiti. I guess she did it to try to cover the scar, but you could still see it peeking through.

"Rule #2 – Raise your hand to speak. I am very interested in what you have to say, but we can't all be speaking out whenever we want, can we? So, to answer your question, Miss – your name?"

"Brittney. Like Britney Spears, but I use two 't's," she said shyly.

There was loud laughter throughout the room. "Dream on, girl. Dream on," Roberto burst out. "You no closer to Britney Spears than a dog is a cat."

Brittney turned to Roberto like a snake about to attack its prey, "Who you think you are, you Cuban wanna-be? You think you all bad with your silver chains and stuff. Shoooot. You ain't nothin'."

Roberto leaped up out of his seat and said threateningly to Brittney, "Don't try me like that, oooh, you just try – don't try me like that Haitian mama."

Mr. Martin took one step in the direction of Roberto and said in an almost-growl, "Excuse me, we don't call each other names in this class."

"And I suppose that's rule #3." I couldn't believe it came out of my mouth. But since I suddenly had a captive audience, I found myself saying, "Well, Mr. Martin, you must think you got some other class, because we here – we're the misfits – we're not like any other class with **rules** and such." There, I had said it, and I really don't know where it had come from. But, in a way I was glad I had said it. I do have a certain rep to keep up – a combination of the smart-aleck, come-back kid with a reputation of doing the least amount of work possible to pass and get out of school.

"No rules, huh?" Mr. Martin addressed his question to me.

"That's right. You see, in this class, we don't do a whole lot of work, so there's no need for a lot of rules. We play cards, play pencil wars, listen to CDs, because as long as we keep quiet and stay out of everyone's trouble, we're doing what the principal wants us to."

"Your principal, Dr. Penny Thornton? The same Dr. Thornton that hired me?" Mr. Martin asked.

"That's right," Markus added in. He was coming to my side now that Mr. Martin was starting to see what our class was about. "You see there's just us 12. And as long as we stay in this room all day and don't go messin' with the other kids, you know getting in fights, throwing stink bombs, you know that kind of stuff, then she's happy. So like Marvin says, we don't need a lot of rules."

"Except for the Uno rules," Luis added in. Luis was from the Dominican-Republic and had a rich, deep cocoa-colored skin color. He wore his hair short on top and had an eager look to his face. "Every time we play Uno, Mike tries to cheat. So we do need to get another set of Uno rules."

"Do not," Mike blurted, and cuffed Luis toward the side of his head.

"Do too," Luis said, as he returned the cuff to Mike.

"HEY! Knock it off!" Mr. Martin said. "Well, I hate to be the one to burst your bubble, but that same principal who hired me has quite a different plan for this class. This year, the State of Florida is going to be grading all schools from A to F on the end of the year tests in reading and math and writing. You – each and every one of you – are very important to making our school get a good grade. Not only will it be based on how well you do, but also if you improve over last year's reading and math scores. From the preliminary information Dr. Thornton has given me, it looks like only 1 or 2 of you are on grade level for reading and math, and many of you are on like a 5th or 6th grade reading level."

"It don't matter," Danielle said. "The teacher always gives us a good grade anyway, so they can pass us to the next grade. I don't think they really want us here any more," she added, with a giggle.

"But it DOES matter," Mr. Martin said. "And YOU matter to me. I'm specially trained in writing, so that's why they want me to prepare you for the very rigorous essay writing exam in February."

There was a simultaneous groan throughout the room.

He continued without losing a beat, "All eighth graders must take this writing exam to pass onto high school, and you must score at least a "3" out of 6 possible points. I'm going to teach you all about sentence structure, transitions, organization, impressive vocabulary, and much more. And, yes, to do that, this class will have rules."

Another collective groan went out over the room.

After a long pause of silence for effect, Mr. Martin looked into our eyes and said, "Who believes in miracles?"

Beljania offered, "You mean like that movie *The Miracle Worker*, where that girl can't see or hear or talk?" When no one answered her, Beljania added, "Remember, that was the movie the substitute played for us last year?" A few of us nodded our heads.

Mr. Martin continued, "Yes, something like that. When something happens that is totally a miracle, something that no one could ever imagine happening, then that is a miracle.

"Like I began, you and me, we're a team. I'm your coach and your teacher and we're going to be working on some miracles this year. Are you ready to join me?"

I, Marvin McDonald, was not going to be suckered into this "rah, rah, go, team, go" junk that was just a come on to make us do all these boring worksheets, tests and book reading. I kept my silent protests to myself, as I was sure a lot of other kids did too.

"Mr. Martin?"

"Yes, miss? Your name? I will learn them all once I get a seating chart."

"Assigned seats?" groaned Mike. "No way."

"Quinesha."

"Yes, Quinesha, you had a question?"

"Yes, Mr. Martin. Mr. Martin, when do we go to lunch?"

Chapter 4
The Power of the Pen

They say you can train a puppy to be dodo-trained in about two weeks, and I guess that's about how long it took Mr. Martin to "train" us misfits with all of his "rules." First came the assigned seats, which wasn't too bad because I got a seat in the third row, next to Markus. As for Rule #2, raise your hand to speak, well we do that some of the time, but more often than not, someone always has to just blurt out something like when Beljania jumped up and said she just haaad to go to the bathroom, and it was a girl thing and that's all anybody needed to know about that! I mean, girls have it made. I think they use that "girl thing" excuse way too much, beyond the laws of biology! I mean, I think Beljania had that same excuse last year about 4 or 5 times a month! As for Rule #3, don't call each other names, well, Mr. Martin sure has his work cut out for himself. Middle school kids love to call each other names, like when Danielle told Mike, "You so ugly," and he retorted, "At least I ain't no cow." It seems like someone is always calling someone some kind of a name, whether it's "wanna-be", mama's boy, Haitian mama, loser, freak, nothing, dumb, stupid, retarded ... the list is endless. Mr. Martin's statements that, "Let's show mutual respect toward each other," and "Treat others like you want to be treated," seem to have gone in one side of our heads and out the other. Well, I guess some puppies take longer to get **fully** trained, and I guess that's us.

One of the biggest changes in our classroom is the way it looks. Mr. Martin actually hung up an American flag, so now we have to say the pledge first thing in the morning, just like all the other kids in school. We also get to watch MTV (that's Monty Middle School TV) every morning because Mr. Martin attached the cable to our TV in the correct way. (We never did watch it at all last year because our teacher never bothered to hook it up.) We all like watching the morning anchors and love making fun of them, the way they look, and the way they talk.

But then the strangest thing begins after morning TV. We actually do school work!

Not just busy work, mind you. But Mr. Martin has us doing some pretty cool stuff. He made us an official schedule where we have regular classes each hour. Writing first, usually some type of journal writing or something. He's always telling us that "The Power of The Pen is Mightier Than The Sword," whatever that means. I mean who uses a sword any more anyways? Then reading, lots of reading because he says we have to go up at least two grade levels in reading for those end-of-the-year tests. So far, that's been pretty cool, because instead of just making us read silently by ourselves, we act out plays and stand up in front of the class and read aloud. So far, we did a version of "Tom Sawyer" where Huck has a dead cat. We could barely get through that part of the play, everyone was howling with laughter, even Nicole, who is usually so quiet. Luis, who had been playing Huck, took a furry skin Mr. Martin had brought in and was pretending it was the dead cat. He kept shoving it at Quinesha, who was playing Becky, and she was getting so mad.

"You shove that thing at me one more time, I'll kick you where the sun don't shine," she growled at him.

Meanwhile, the class was roaring, while Mr. Martin was saying, "Let's keep it down, now, keep it down."

Then, we have lunch, 12:15- 12:40 p.m. – a mere 25 minutes. Man, do people running schools think we just like inhale our food? No wonder people get indigestion! Especially people like me. You see, I'm a big guy. Well, not my height exactly, which seems to have topped right now at 5'2". But I'm big – about 155 pounds. So I need a lot of food and you need time to eat a lot of food. I usually get two pieces of pizza, a French fry, a couple of chocolate chip cookies and chocolate milk. Is it any wonder that my stomach is a little upset when we have to come back to class and do math? I'm not particularly fond of math anyway, and it's a lot of just doing problems from the book, which I hate.

Luckily, by the time math is over, my lunch is usually digested enough for me to get into social studies and science. Mr. Martin has us taping together this great big plastic bubble house that's supposed to be like a space station or something. He says when it's done, we're going to go outside on the field and fill it with air. He even wants the MTV guys to videotape it. No way do I want to be on TV. I have a reputation to maintain, like I said, doing the least amount of schoolwork and passing.

So today we're making a time capsule to go with this space theme. We're supposed to write about our past, present and future and then Mr. Martin is going to lock them up in a capsule and we'll open it at the end of the year to see how we've changed. I know I won't change! I hate change. Change hurts. Like my past. Okay, before I write, I'm going to "brainstorm," just like Mr. Martin told us. Pretend there's a storm in our brain and shoot around a bunch of different ideas to get inspiration to write. My past, well it hadn't been too bad until mom and dad split up. Dad and I did everything together – he coached my football team, my baseball team, except that was when I was ten. Then mom decided she wanted a divorce and she was moving back up north to be with her relatives and she said dad could keep me here in Florida. I mean change hurts. It was like she didn't even want me, just like if someone was giving a puppy away at the dog pound or something. Dad was pretty upset, because he hadn't really wanted the divorce, but he was happy because he and I would still be together. Until he started to get lonely. I guess it was another two years before he "fell in love" with a mom who had a boy on our football team. She also was divorced and had three other kids. She had been married to a doctor and was pretty well off. I had been to her home a few times and even got along with the boy who was about my same age, Travis, but she started telling dad that things were missing after I had been in the house. She said that Travis' expensive gold initial was missing and asked him to ask me if I had taken it. Man, that put a wedge between me and my dad. I guess he wanted to believe me when I said that I never took any stupid jewelry (I mean why would I want a "T" initial letter?), but he stopped taking me with him when he went over there. Then, he started to spend the night over there two to three times a week, until he decided to move in with her. Even though dad built an addition to her back porch, which was supposed to be my room, she (Teresa) turned it into a rec room for her four kids, complete with a fooz-ball game, computer, large screen TV, and other electronic goodies. She put a mattress up in the loft and said I was to sleep up there. She liked to have her house nice and tidy, so the first time I did sleep there in the loft it wasn't too bad except that someone had taken away the steps to climb down the loft. I hollered and hollered until Travis sauntered in and said, "What are you screaming about?" "Hey, nut-head, put the ladder up here so I can get down." He just laughed at me and laughed at me. He thought it was hilarious me perched up there like some darn bird in a cage or something. Finally, he put up the ladder and I went down as fast as I could and just slugged him. He ticked me off so bad. He ran crying to Teresa, who complained to my dad that this living arrangement might just not work out.

After that, I pretty much stayed over at Markus' house. He was an only child and his parents had a nice big house. His mom was a nurse, so she wasn't home because she worked from 3 p.m. – 11 p.m. His dad worked construction and he often stayed out after work with his friends for a few beers at the local bar. So they were happy that Markus had someone with him after school. We told them we needed to do our homework together, and they bought it!

Instead, we usually opened up a can of Spaghetti and Meatballs or Raviolis and warmed them up in the microwave and played Playstation 2 games for hours. Many times, we'd fall asleep in front of the TV.

As I said before, change hurts. Sure, staying over at Markus' house wasn't bad, but I have to admit, I do miss my dad. What makes it even worse is that he is now like a second daddy to Teresa's kids. Teresa has my dad driving her kids to their private schools in the morning and afternoon and running them places after school, too. I guess her "surgically enhanced" figure and blond curls have a hold on him that even his own son can't compete with.

Okay, Mr. Martin, my past. How much of this do you want me to write? Do you even care, or is this just busywork to keep us all quiet. Do I even want to read this in the spring when you open the Time Capsule?

I wrote, "My Past. Nothing much to write about. My mom and dad got divorced when I was 10. My mom moved back to Chicago to be with her relatives. My dad moved in with his girlfriend and her four kids. I flunked 7th grade and can't wait to make it out of this sorry school." Like I said, brief and to the point. What's the use of wasting a lot of words on writing?

Chapter 5
Can a Leopard Change Its Spots?

There's an old saying that a leopard can't change its spots, and I guess that means that you can't change how a person really is. I don't know if that's true or not, because in some ways our class – which is definitely not your normal class – is changing. For example, just yesterday, during our morning routine when we have to say the pledge to our American Flag and then watch Monty T.V., you could hear at least 4 voices reciting the Pledge of Allegiance like this, "I pledge allegiance to the flag, of the United States of America, and to the republic for which it stands, one HAITIAN, under God, Indivisible, with Liberty and Justice for all." It all started a few weeks ago when

Mike told some of the boys this story, "This one little Haitian boy went to school for the first time in America and he didn't know the Pledge of Allegiance. He thought the word "Nation" was "Haitian." So the dumb kid said, 'One HAITIAN under God...' Can you believe it?" Mike wasn't exactly known for his appreciation of other cultures. Sure, he hung out with Hispanics like Roberto, Luis and Jesus, but he didn't really care to hang with Markus, which is cool by me because Markus is my dog.

Anyway, since that time, Mike, Roberto, Luis, and Jesus always said the pledge that way and then Brittney (who is actually our only student from Haiti) joined in, like she was proud to say it or something. Then, Roberto started to say, "One CUBAN under God," and Luis started to say, "One DOMINICAN REPUBLIC under God," and Jesus started to say, "One PUERTO RICAN under God." It sounded like a symphony with all those different voices. Like I said, our class just ain't like the normal kids.

Mr. Martin didn't say anything the first few times, but then yesterday, in our reading hour, we had to read a couple of books. One was on pride and respect for other cultures and nationalities. Then we read this really short book called "The Children's Story," by James Clavell. That was one cool book, I mean the whole book took place in just 45 minutes and it was about how this new teacher persuaded the students to cut up their flag and give up all their beliefs. It was supposed to be on how propaganda can be used to tear up our nation. A lot of us were pretty shocked by that book. So today, when Mike blurted out loud as ever, "One HAITIAN under God," there weren't as many voices joining him. Amazingly, the rest of the voices were saying, "One nation under God." So maybe leopards can change their spots. Maybe change doesn't always hurt.

Also, Mr. Martin had said yesterday, "I see many of you take great pride in the country you are originally from, whether it's Cuba, Dominican Republic, Mexico, Haiti, or even the United States. Today we are going to start a new exciting unit on Family Tree, where we will research our ancestors and the countries they are from and share our discoveries with the class." Then he had us break up into groups of three and make up Jazz Chants on the topic of Family Tree. (Mr. Martin is big on Jazz Chants. He brought in these bongo drums and has one of us beat along to something he's trying to teach us. Uusually it's Spaz Ron because he really likes to beat those drums and

I think Mr. Martin wants to try to get him out of his little shell.)

Anyway, I really liked the jazz chant me, Markus and Ron made up. It went like this:

Family tree, family tree
It always starts with Little Ol' Me

A mother, a father,
My grandparents too
Let's get to know them
Starting with "Who."

My mother's mother is my maternal grandmother,
My father's father is my paternal grandfather.
Let's not forget our uncles and aunts,
Now I hope you can remember
With Our funny lil' chant!

But when we had to go in front of the class to recite our chant, we changed the last two lines to:

But it really all started when good old dad
Got into my dear sweet Mom's underpants!

The class was howling with laughter when we said the surprise ending, and even Mr. Martin couldn't hide a laugh. That was totally cool. It's very cool when you are so funny in class and everyone thinks you're funny. I mean that definitely raises your status in the class several notches. I received some very appreciative looks from all the girls, too, especially Danielle.

Chapter 6
D.O.P. on M.T.V.

Do you like to gamble and bet? I do; it gives me a rush, especially when I win. But if someone would have given me the chance to bet on the event I was watching on M.T.V. right now, I wouldn't have taken that long-shot in a million years. I mean, who could have predicted that our misfit D.O.P. class would be on M.T.V. (Monty Middle School Television)? But here we were, as our class watched in silent amazement.

"This is Sheila Thompson of M.T.V., broadcasting live from our athletic fields with Mr. Martin's 8th grade class." The TV screen was filled with Sheila Thompson and Mr. Martin. You could see the rest of us 12 kids behind them. "Mr. Martin, what exactly do we have here that your class created?"

"Ms. Thompson, have you ever wondered what it would be like to live in a space ship atmosphere, totally cut off from earth's atmosphere? Well, my class has created a bubble-house, if you will, that is totally free from the Earth's atmosphere."

Then the video showed our 15' x 9' "house" made up entirely with huge plastic sheets, which our class taped together with extra strong adhesive tape. The front of our creation had a door with a flap through which we guys walked into the "house." It was inflated by a single box fan, which Mr. Martin had plugged into an extension cord and into a nearby electrical outlet. He allowed six of us at a time to enter the house, and it was a feeling I'll never forget.

It was a feeling of breathing this very pure air that felt different than other air. As I looked around at the other kids in there with me – Markus, Jesus, Nicole, Danielle and Ron – I could see looks on their faces that seemed to say that they were feeling the same way I was about this. It linked us together in a way I can't really explain. But I have to admit that the coolest part was that we made it ourselves and that now all the school would see it and they would think it was cool, too.

"And here we have our principal, Dr. Thornton, entering the spaceship atmosphere, along with eighth grade dean, Mr. Tonell," announced Sheila Thompson. The video zoomed up to close-ups of their faces, which you could see through the plastic. Someone started to laugh and others joined in, but Quinesha said loudly, "SSShhhhh," and it was quiet in the class again.

"Well, there you have it, a scientific creation by Mr. Martin's eighth grade class." You could see the 12 of us around the student reporter. Luis was putting bunny ears on Beljania. "You are sooo stupid, you know that," Beljania shouted at Luis, but again Quinesha said, "SSShhhh."

"And I'm Sheila Thompson for M.T.V." The video portion was over and a picture of the American flag was on the screen.

"Bravo," Mr. Martin said proudly and began clapping. Soon everyone was clapping. When we all stood up that day to say the pledge, it seemed that we all said it a little more in unison, more clearly and without missing a beat. "One nation, under God ..."

Chapter 7
Marvin gets Muscle

Everyone was working on their "All About Me" books for our Family Tree Unit, where we had to do like 10 different things and compile them in a book. It involved our past, present and future. I have to admit, it did get me thinking.

"Mr. Martin, do you lift weights?" I asked my teacher, who was sitting at his desk grading some papers.

"Yes, I do Marvin. Why do you ask?"

The scene by the bus yesterday flashed through my mind. "Hey, bubble boy," Freddie Crooper called out to me as I was getting on the bus to go home with Markus. "You looked so fat on TV, I'm surprised you fit into that freak plastic thing you and your other losers made. Bubble boy in a bubble house," he called out, loudly, calling attention to himself. A lot of kids around him started laughing and I heard a few kids say, "Bubble boy."

"Oh, I guess I just wanted to work out a little, you know, maybe lose a little weight."

"Sure, but working out is just half the solution. Diet is extremely important. Food is really fuel for your body. Do you know much about fat grams and that kind of stuff?"

"Oh, I hate that fat-free junk. Tastes like cardboard."

"I'm not talking about commercial fat-free foods. Just foods that are naturally low in fat, like vegetables, fruits, lean meats like turkey, whole grain breads."

"I usually just eat the pizza, french fries, chocolate milk and cookies at lunch."

"Well, that's a great place to start then. Instead of that, why not try the sub sandwich they offer in the regular food line?"

"I wouldn't dare go in that line. It's for all the poor kids that get free lunch. I go into the fast food line."

"Well, if you want muscle, you need to start with the proper foods. Now I don't think the regular food line is just for poor kids, do you? You could get a sub sandwich, a salad and a piece of fruit. They even have low-fat 1% milk."

Yuck, I thought to myself. I hate white milk. "Uh, oh, thanks anyway Mr. Martin," I said, as I started back for my seat.

"Wait," Mr. Martin said. "You asked me about working out and I never really answered your question. I do work out, usually before work. I do bicep work with 5 pound hand weights, tricep work, and a lot of abdominal work, crunches and sit-ups. I jog about 4 mornings, about 2 miles each run. Makes me feel great."

"What's the difference between a bicep and tricep?" I asked.

"I'll tell you what Marvin, I've been trying to think of a new topic for our math and science area and I think nutrition and muscle structure would be a great topic. Do you ever read the labels on cans of food?"

"No way, I'm lucky if I got the energy to just open the can, pour the food in a bowl, microwave it and eat it," I said.

"Well, we can calculate our math problems using nutrition labels. We can compare calories, fat grams, cholesterol, and other facts. Thanks Marvin for a great idea."

"No problem," I said, as I once again went for my seat.

"Hey, Marv, I have an extra set of weights at home. Would you like to borrow them, if I bring them into class?"

"For sure, thanks," I muttered. I wanted to say something like, "You're the best Mr. Martin. You're not like any other teacher I've ever had; you actually care about us," but these words just stayed in my mind. I couldn't wait until tomorrow when I would receive my first weights. I'd show Freddie that "Bubble Boy" could turn into "Muscle Marvin." I'd show him, all right.

Chapter 8
Mr. Martin's Secret Past

Is it possible that I am really enjoying coming to school? But it's not only me, it's all 12 of us, well, maybe 11 of us because Nicole is absent about 2 – 3 times a week. I feel sad when I look at her with that white powdered makeup on and those black lips. I hate to admit it, but she seems to have an odor to her, too, like a musty not-clean smell. I had heard that she has a pretty bad home life; her mother is like about 300 pounds and supposedly slaps Nicole whenever she gets mad about something, Last year, the seventh grade dean had to pick up the mother and drive her to school for a parent conference because she can't drive. It was rumored that Nicole was living on the streets last year because her mom had a boyfriend move in with her and Nicole hated him. The story went that he slapped Nicole and she slapped him back, and then she walked out the door with just the clothes on her back. She was out of school for weeks until they finally caught up with her. She had been living on the streets and almost got raped by this bunch of drunken men. I guess that's when she went into a store and shoplifted some food and the police came and the whole story came out. She was sent back to her house and now she was back in school. She didn't talk much, but our middle school is like a soap opera. Everyone seems to know everything about everyone.

But like I was saying, all of us were really having fun in school and learning a lot, too. It was almost Christmas vacation and our big Writing Test was in February, so we were writing a 5-paragraph essay every day. Now, I have to admit, I always HATED writing. To me, what's the use of a lot of words on a page when a few words say the same thing? But Mr. Martin told us that to get a really high score – a 6 was the highest that almost no one ever got – that we needed to do specific things. First, we needed to focus on the topic. In other words, if they ask you who your hero is, you can't talk about your summer vacation. That would be "off topic." Then, we learned about essay structure. Mr. Martin taught us this very-weird chant, that went like this:

One little, two little, three little reasons

Writing my expository this season,

Introduction, Body, Conclusion,

I know how to write, that's not an allusion.

I know how to write, that's not an allusion.

I have to admit, even though it sounded like a kindergarten song, it made me remember that my essays had to have an introduction, a body with three supporting reasons and a conclusion.

Mr. Martin did EVERYTHING he could to get us excited about this essay test. One day, he brought in this really off-the-chain fishing pole with a huge magnet on it. He had 5 different "fish" that the pole would attract. He had explained that we need to "hook" our readers with a catchy beginning sentence in our introduction. Some of the "hooks" we could use were a question, a startling fact, a statistic, a brief story or anecdote. He said a good beginning could turn our essay from a mere passing score of "3" to a "5" or even a "6."

On another day, Mr. Martin brought in a real hamburger, a Whopper actually. He said we needed to structure our essays like a hamburger with a beginning (the top bun), a middle (the meat) and a conclusion (the bottom bun.) He explained that the middle would be very plain if it didn't have some extra stuff on it like cheese, ketchup and a pickle. He told us that the middle was our three reasons and that we needed to expand our ideas to get a good score. Then, he pulled out a package of French fries. (I have to admit, this was getting me hungry. I had been following Mr. Martin's advice about lunch and working out with the weights and already had lost about 5 pounds, but this aroma from the burger and fries was getting me really hungry.)

"You must support your essays with fries," Mr. Martin said as he wrote F.R.I.E.S. on the board. Under each letter, Mr. Martin wrote out something that we were supposed to use in our body paragraphs. It looked like this:

F.	R.	I.	E.	S.
Facts	Reasons	Incidents	Examples	Statistics

Mr. Martin had also taught us to use descriptive words ("Don't say something is good, say it is "marvelous" "spectacular" "extraordinary"); he taught us to use big vocabulary words (such as "vehemently.") For example, at the end of your persuasive essay, you write, "I vehemently urge you to consider..." or something like that. In case you don't know, vehemently means strongly.

Then, we learned all about similes. Mr. Martin had us make a big picture book about animal fur and each one of us had to write a simile about how animals' skins feel. Our finished book included stuff like, "Porcupine skin feels like prickly needles," "Rabbit fur feels like soft velvet," "Pig skin feels like a coarse hair brush." In case you didn't know, similes are when two unlike things are compared using like or as.

Mr. Martin would grade our essays every day. Most of us were already getting the passing grade of "3," but some of us had received 4's, a few 5's, but no 6's. I was really surprised when I received my first 5. It was on the persuasive topic, "What would you change about the cafeteria food in your school and why?" Maybe it was because I had used the word, vehemently, I don't know. But, to be truthful, I do feel I'm becoming a better writer, and it's a really good feeling. It makes you think about what Mr. Martin says, "The power of the pen is mightier than the sword."

All of us knew Mr. Martin was a great writer, and we had all wondered why he would have left a great job of being a writer to come teach the likes of us, but no one had the guts to ask him such a personal question. Except for Quinesha. Quinesha and her "tag-team" partner Beljania have the guts to ask things no one else would.

"Mr. Martin," Quinesha began. "Why are you a teacher when you're a great writer?"

"To help you guys ace that test in February," he answered.

"No, really," added Beljania. "I mean we all know beginning teachers don't make that much money, especially in Florida, but writers do. Why did you quit your job at that great magazine where you used to work?"

"To be honest, I'll share something with you, with this class. I don't want it going any farther than this class, right. Can I trust you?" Mr. Martin looked at us, and everyone quietly nodded their heads up and down.

"It's human nature to be jealous of someone when they're doing great and you're not doing so great. That doesn't make it right, mind you, but it is human nature. Well, that's what happened at my job. I was doing great. I was the top reporter with more Page One stories than any other writer. I was making $65,000 a year doing what I loved. But then I was working on this really controversial story that involved a lot of government officials and it got messy. People that I worked with started to say that I was making up my sources just to get the big story. Then, I was sued by this town manager for libel because he denied his quote. It went to court and everything and I lost because I couldn't produce the tape that I had recorded our conversation on. Wouldn't you have known, my tape player hadn't been working right that day and when I went to retrieve my notes, it was blank. But I had written the story anyway, just using my notes. Luckily, the insurance at the magazine paid the legal damages, but I wanted no more of that career. When people turn against you, it's not worth it."

We were all shocked that Mr. Martin had told us such personal details about his life. It made us look at him in a different way, not just as a teacher, but also as a person too.

But like I said before, middle school kids just love to talk. Our middle school is like a soap opera.

Everyone seems to know everything about everyone, and Mr. Martin's story was no exception.

Chapter 9
Tree of Life

We were all hyper because it was the last day before winter break. That meant two whole weeks off – we had the week off before Christmas and the week off after Christmas. So today our class was having a little party. Well, in middle school you can't have "parties," you have to call them "success celebrations." Mr. Martin even brought in a big sheet cake with "Success Celebration" inscribed on it. All of us kids brought in some type of snack to share, and there were bags of chips, cookies, candy, soda – a regular feast.

"So what are we celebrating?" Brittney asked Mr. Martin.

"We're celebrating your success. Most of you now know how to write a very good essay and the recent computer tests we took showed that most of you have made great reading and math gains. A lot of you are now on grade level, and that's what we're celebrating."

I felt bad watching Mr. Martin talk so proudly of us. He really did care for us; in fact, we almost seemed like a family. So why did I feel badly? Because –like I said before middle school kids just love to talk – now the whole school knew about Mr. Martin's past at the magazine. Except, well you know how the truth gets twisted the more gossip is passed around? Now the final story goes something like this: Mr. Martin lied and cheated his way to the top beating out all other reporters for the top stories. In fact, he made up damaging quotes of a respected good politician, and the quotes were all lies. He had to go to court (some versions of the story even say he was in jail) and lost and it cost the magazine a lot of money, so they fired him.

Now I felt that somehow our class had turned against him, and he didn't deserve it. It seemed like the other teachers didn't really bother to talk to him much. You could see it at lunchtime when the teachers come to pick up their classes. Mr. Martin walked up to a few teachers the other day, and they just seemed to ignore him. I don't know who started passing the story around, probably the girls, they gossip more than boys. But I know it wasn't ME.

Mr. Martin just kept going on in this positive way he has (kind of like the Energizer bunny); if fact, we were on M.T.V. again. So maybe the other teachers are just jealous of him because he comes up with these really cool projects that we do. Our last big project was a giant TREE OF LIFE that we created on the school wall just outside our classroom. All of us traced our handprints on green construction paper and then decorated them with glitter. Mr. Martin told us to make our hands very individual, reflecting our personalities. Then, he had the principal and deans and other important people at our school trace their hands in brown construction paper. Together, our class constructed a giant tree with the green hands forming the branches and the brown hands forming the trunk and roots. Then, around the tree we put samples of our class work that went along with the theme of "roots." For example, we had done vocabulary work studying the meanings of various roots, such as "migra" means "to move." Mr. Martin says that we can figure out almost any word if we know what the roots, prefixes and suffixes mean. We also did math with square roots and studied history with the video series "Roots." Since the TREE OF LIFE was the grand finale of our Family Tree unit, it was also surrounded by our posters we created about our heritage.

Dr. Thornton had been so impressed, she had put the whole thing on M.T.V., and I have to admit, it did look really great. I can't believe I had NEVER done anything like this in all my previous years of school. No wonder I never really liked school before now.

I never really thought that anything you learned in school could actually change your life for the better. But that was before I met Mr. Martin. You know how I told you Mike always had some stupid comment to say about people's races and stuff? I mean, you could have called him racist before. Well, now all that's changed.

It was like this slow evolution of something. For weeks, each person in our class talked about things in their family tree, like where they were from, their family, foods they eat, and customs. Slowly, there was more talking among all of us. Mike was even joking around with Markus, and even Spaz Ron (except now we pretty much have dropped the "Spaz" part) has come out of his shell and is talking to people.

But one of the biggest changes is with Nicole. This week, she came to school for the first time with just her normal skin tone and lips, minus the white makeup and black lipstick. I mean, it was a shock! She looked totally different. Even though Nicole never said much, it was known that she didn't get along with people of other races, probably because of her mom and stuff. Well, at our school, which is located in Southeast Florida, we have kids from every imaginable country such as Costa Rica, Puerto Rico, Jamaica, Haiti, Dominican Republic, Peru, Cuba, and Mexico. Our racial mix is about 1/3 white, 1/3 Hispanic, 1/3 Black, and for most kids, like me, it's not a problem. Never has been. But it was like really a miracle seeing people like Nicole, Mike and Ron changing. Very strange indeed.

Like I said, we were hyper because it was our "Success Celebration." I couldn't wait for the 4 p.m. bell to ring so I could start my Christmas vacation, even if it meant spending it in Teresa's home. I missed my dad and decided that I would definitely be with him this holiday.

Chapter 10
Life is Like a Roller Coaster

For me, life is like a roller coaster. Whenever I'm at a high, I come flying down to a new low. It's funny, ever since Mr. Martin taught us about similes, I think of everything in similes. Did you know that Forest Gump's famous saying "Life is Like a Box of Chocolates" is a simile?

But even though life is like a roller coaster because it has highs and lows, it's not fun like a roller coaster. So I guess a more accurate simile would be "My life is like a BAD roller coaster ride."

Let me explain. I was like so ready for Christmas vacation. I had been in such a good mood. School had been really tight, and we were actually becoming like celebrities at the school from being on M.T.V. so much. We had so much fun that last day in school, eating the "Success Celebration" cake, munching on all the food. I admit, I did eat a lot that day, but did I tell you? I have been working out with the barbells Mr. Martin gave me and doing abdominal crunches for weeks now, and even though I weigh the same, well even a little more but you know muscle weighs more than fat, I look really good. I did shoot up 4 inches, which everyone says is typical for 8th grade boys, so now I'm 5'6" and I weigh 165. I don't look like "bubble boy" any more.

Like I said, I was really pumped for Christmas vacation with my dad – even if it meant spending it at Teresa's home. The days before Christmas Eve weren't all that bad. Did I tell you that Teresa has four kids? Her one daughter, Sandra, is grown and she goes to FSU in Tallahassee. She didn't come home until Christmas Eve. Then, she has Taylor, who is a junior in high school. Taylor has her own car, goes to the preppy high school near Teresa's luxurious home, and is very spoiled. She has a huge closet in her bedroom with row after row of color-coordinated clothes with shoes to match! Compared to my wardrobe, I'm like dog-crap. I mean I have like maybe 4 school shirts, 2 pairs of good jeans, and some other stuff, but most of it is not designer label or anything. When dad and

I went shopping for school clothes at Wal-Mart, we were done in about 20 minutes.

Teresa's third child is the boy who played on my dad's football team, Travis. Travis and I get along pretty good, but he is also majorly spoiled. He's also in eighth grade, but he goes to the middle school in the classy part of town, the one where all the kids get good test scores and awards and all that. The parents of these kids are doctors, lawyers, business people, managers, not like the parents of the kids at my school, who are landscape workers, restaurant workers, housekeepers, laundromat workers, construction workers. But, lately, I wouldn't change places with my school and my friends at school for anything.

Last but definitely not least is Teresa's fourth child, Tiffany, who if I had to compare her to someone, I would say she is like the female version of Dudley from *Harry Potter.* Tiffany is in sixth grade and overindulges – (notice I use big words now. Mr. Martin said higher level vocabulary increases your power) – in everything. She overindulges in eating, consumption of video games and TV, and has to be first at everything. Whenever she doesn't get her way, she cuddles up to her mom and says, "I'm the baby of the family, so you have to spoil me more than the others."

Like I said, I was pumped to spend Christmas vacation at Teresa's home. I thought it might actually be pretty cool, playing video games with Travis and staying up late watching TV. I was even ready to sleep in my loft and was determined to somehow figure out a way to keep the ladder up there so I could go up and down as I wanted.

But, my first surprise was when I looked up at my loft bed area, and it was filled to the brim with wrapped Christmas packages! There was no way even a mouse would have room to sleep up there!

Teresa had just shook her blond curls and said to me, "We weren't sure you would be here for the holidays with us, Marvin, so I hope you don't mind. I used that area to store Christmas presents. I guess I just ran out of room under the tree." Then she muttered more to herself than to me, "Maybe I did go a little overboard, but thank God for MasterCard! You can sleep on this couch if you want."

"That's fine," I answered politely. I was determined not to get into it with Teresa. I wanted to ask why I couldn't just sleep upstairs where all the other bedrooms were, maybe on the floor in Travis' room on a sleeping bag or something, but I figured Teresa probably thought I had cooties or something.

The next surprise was seeing my dad as the next Mr. Mom. Dad's job is fixing engines on race cars and things like that, so he has a pretty flexible schedule. Teresa works at a real estate office, so she is on the road a lot in her Mercedes, showing clients properties. Before she leaves for work, she has a whole schedule of stuff for dad to do. Like on Dec. 22, dad had to drive Tiffany to her dance recital practice at 3 p.m. and then pick her up at 4:30 p.m. Then, he usually makes the dinner for us kids –usually something like pizza, spaghetti, hot dogs or hamburgers. Later, after Teresa has taken her bath in her spa-like bathtub, he cooks another dinner for him and Teresa, like salad, steak, salmon, shrimp – things like that so Teresa can keep her "10" figure (which as I said before has definitely been surgically enhanced!) Or, they go out to eat at a restaurant, which is like about 3 times a week. I don't know where my dad is getting all his money. I mean, he probably makes about $45,000 a year and I know he had some savings, but I think this romance with Teresa must be cleaning him out. But, if dad is happy, I'm happy. Or at least I tried to be until the day after Christmas.

Chapter 11
Surviving the Holidays

Somehow I survived Christmas. It wasn't easy when Teresa's kids opened present after expensive present while I basically watched. I guess I don't have a rich doctor father like they do, a mother whose second home is the mall, and rich doting grandparents. It wasn't like I was totally ignored – dad did buy me some new clothes, and even a silver chain with an M initial letter – but I definitely felt like an outsider during the whole ordeal.

Would you believe that my mom sent me nothing? She wrote me and my dad a letter "sending her love for Christmas" and wrote that money was very tight now because she was expecting a baby! Imagine that! She couldn't afford me and she didn't want me, but she decided to have a baby with some guy she met in Chicago. That letter left me with a very strange feeling.

Teresa has the kids open presents on Christmas Eve. She says it works out better that way because she videotapes the whole event like it's a movie or something and that way everyone is dressed in their fine holiday clothes. I always liked it at my house when mom and dad were still married because we opened our presents on Christmas morning. Everyone would be in their pajamas and mom would be sipping her coffee and there would be some danish rolls to eat and everyone was happy and relaxed. What had happened to change all that?

"Look here, Tiffany," Teresa called out while wielding the video camcorder. "What did Santa bring you, Tiffany?"

Tiffany batted her eyelashes at the video camera. "I received all sorts of wonderful presents from Santa. That's because I'm so good, I get the most presents."

I couldn't help but snort under my breath.

"I received these wonderful clothes from money from Pappa and Gramma, thank you Pappa and Gramma. I received this gorgeous 14K gold chain necklace from Mom."

"Don't forget to thank Tom, too," Teresa added, referring to my dad.

I thought to myself, dad pitched in money to buy Tiffany that expensive necklace? When she is the most spoiled selfish girl in town? I couldn't believe it.

Was it my imagination or did Tiffany give me a spiteful look before turning to my dad and saying, "Thank you, Tom. It's truly lovely." She dangled the necklace in front of the camcorder. Man, that necklace was thick. That thing must have cost $400 at least.

Teresa repeated this ritual with all of her children, and one by one they showed off their new presents, thanking their grandparents, things like that. Probably Teresa makes up a copy of the tape and sends it to "Pappa and Gramma."

Teresa was about to put the camcorder away when my dad gave her this look, and she said in her somewhat-fake way she has of talking, "Let's not forget Marvin. Good gracious no. I guess I'm just not used to Marvin being here, that's all. So what did Santa bring you, Marvin?"

I was so embarrassed. The boxes around me looked so sorry compared to the ones Teresa's "golden children" had received, all I could say is, "I don't like to talk on camcorders," while putting up my hand at the same time.

"Oh, come on, Marvin. Don't be shy," coaxed Teresa, with her voice all sugary and sweet.

"I'm done here," I said, as I got up and moved to the kitchen to get a drink of water. I could sense the change in the atmosphere in the living room as I left and heard the soft click of the camcorder as Teresa turned it off.

The rest of the evening wasn't so bad because me and Travis played some new Playstation 2 games he had received and Teresa brought out all sorts of desserts. I stuffed myself until I couldn't eat another drop.

Christmas wasn't too bad. Teresa had bought a big Honey Baked Ham, and I think she liked it because she didn't have to cook it. She told us it was to be served at room temperature, because it was fully cooked. She had bought three side dishes to go with it, so all she had to do was microwave them and our dinner was complete. Teresa had nagged at Taylor and Tiffany until they had finally given in and set the table with Teresa's formal china and gold silverware. She even had these gold plates to put under the regular plates, so I have to admit, it did all look really great, and there weren't any problems.

Until Dec. 26. The problem didn't start until the day after Christmas.

Chapter 12
Tiffany's Bedroom

It was the day after Christmas and the atmosphere in the house was pretty mellow. I mean, both my dad and Teresa were at work, Sandra had left early in the morning to go back to FSU, so it was just me, Travis, Taylor and Tiffany at home alone. All of us were raiding the refrigerator, making sandwiches out of the leftover ham, and devouring what was left of the Christmas cookies and desserts. Taylor was getting dressed to go out, but me and Travis just had on these long plaid flannel drawstring pants that Teresa had bought us and t-shirts, and we had no plans on going anywhere except in front of the TV to play Playstation 2 games. Tiffany was watching *The Price is Right* on their large-screen TV.

"69 cents? Are you stupid or something?" Tiffany yelled at the TV set. "That has to be 89 cents at least. Put me on there; I'd win it all. These people are soooo stupid!"

"Hey, Tiffany, keep it down in there. We're trying to play a game in here," Travis called out.

"You aren't my boss. You and Mar-Vin aren't my bosses." Tiffany had this way of saying my name like I was a disgusting foul being or something, accenting the "Mar" of my name and barely pronouncing the "Vin" part.

I just gave her some of her own stuff back. "Tif-fan-y, don't you have some friends to go visit or something so you get out of this house?" I accented the "Tif" part of her name like she says my name, and said "fan-y" like I was referring to a body part!

"Tiffany doesn't have any friends," Travis quipped back to me, smiling. I thought to myself, maybe this won't be too bad. Maybe Travis and I could be like brothers or something.

"I heard that, and it's not funny. I'm going to tell mom that you're being mean to me," Tiffany said, as she stood in the doorway of the rec room. She had this way of slouching so her stomach protruded. She was holding a small plate with a giant piece of chocolate cake on it. Like I said, she reminds me of a female version of Dudley in *Harry Potter.* "I do too have friends," she added, as she huffed back to the TV screen of *The Price is Right.*

"Do you wanna play my new racing video game?" Travis asked me.

"Sure, you got that one?"

"Yeah, I got it for Christmas." Travis ruffled through the various Playstation 2 games on the carpeted floor. "It's not here. Hey, Tiffany, did you borrow my new game?"

Tiffany was standing in the doorway. "What if I did? It's not just yours, you know?" Tiffany had her own Playstation 2 set in her bedroom.

"Oh, yes it is. Mom bought it for me from my money from Pappa and Gramma. Where is it?"

"Oh how special," Tiffany quipped. Tiffany had this annoying way of saying, "Oh how special," after anything you said that's important to you. For example, if I said I got all B's on my report card, she'd say, "Oh, how special" in a sarcastic tone.

"Go get it," Travis told her.

"Okay, I'll get it. Just hold on, I'm in the middle of this cool part of *The Price is Right.*"

"Marvin, go up to Tiffany's room and see if it's up there, okay?" Travis said to me. "I'm going to finish this round."

I leaped up the back stairs to the bedrooms three steps at a time. I hesitated a moment before going into Tiffany's bedroom. I felt strange going into it. I looked around. You know how they decorate the beds in the linen department of major department stores with tons of pillows, feather blankets, and stuff? Well, that's exactly what Tiffany's bed looked like. I mean the bed linens themselves must have cost $500. In fact, her whole room looked like a picture out of a designer book.

I saw where the Playstation 2 game was, on top of her bureau that had these little doors enclosing her TV. As I was ruffling through the games, looking for it, I was surprised by Tiffany's voice that screamed out, "What ARE you DOING in MY ROOM, MAR-vin?"

"Travis told me to get his new video game," I answered meekly. Tiffany's piercing eyes made me feel like I had been doing something vile and wrong.

She shuffled over to her bureau, shoved me out of the way with her pudgy arm and picked up a game.

"Here's his damn game. And I don't EVER want to see you in my room, again. I'm telling mom," Tiffany shouted at me.

"No problem. I'd rather be dead than ever go in your ugly room ever again," I retorted.

"My room, ugly? Well, at least I have a room. Get OUT!"

As I threw the game to Travis, I said, "Next time, you get the game out of your sister's room. She went ballistic on me."

Travis looked uninterested. "Oh, that's just Tiffany. Major drama queen."

"Yeah," I answered, relieved that Travis made it out like it was no big deal. "Yeah, major drama queen," I repeated.

But, unfortunately, it turned out to be a big deal. A very big deal.

Chapter 13
Where is Tiffany's Gold Chain?

About 5 o'clock, my dad arrived back to Teresa's house (I still couldn't call it home) with a big bucket of Kentucky Fried Chicken. He also had cartons of mashed potatoes, gravy and coleslaw. Teresa arrived shortly after. I have to admit, it almost felt like we were a family there for a moment as we all hungrily dug into the chicken and fixings. I wasn't surprised that my dad had paid for everything. He was just that kind of man. I had missed him so much and it felt so good to be around him again, joking and talking.

Dad said, "Hey, Marvo, you got enough chicken there?" My dad often called me "Marvo" when I was younger. He looked at my four pieces of chicken on my plate.

"Yeah, I guess so."

"Teresa, did you notice? Marvin shot up four inches this year and he's been working out. Stretched out a bit and put on some muscle."

Teresa mumbled, "Mmmhmm," seemingly uninterested.

"Mommy," Tiffany said, making her voice sound all babyish. Yuck! "Travis and Mar-vin were mean to me today." She was dabbing one of those wipes around her mouth to pick up the stray pieces of fried chicken.

"We were not," Travis shot back. "She just had the TV on so loud, we couldn't hear our game."

"Well, you all better get along, because there's many more days until you go back to school."

"And Mar-vin was snooping around in my room," Tiffany added, a sly smirk on her face.

"I was not, you little lying thing," the words were out of my mouth before I could stop them.

"Marvin. You cannot talk to Tiffany like that," my father admonished.

"Was to," Tiffany continued. "Snooping through my things and everything."

Teresa looked straight at me. "Why were you in Tiffany's bedroom, Marvin?"

"Travis told me to go get his new video game. Tiffany had it in her room."

"Well, I suggest that we all keep all of our property to ourselves," Teresa said. There was just something about her I didn't like. It was like she looked at everything as "property." No wonder she made such a good real estate agent.

That was all that was said about that until later that night when Tiffany was getting ready to go to bed. She shrieked from her bedroom, "It's GONE. My 14K gold chain necklace is gone!"

Even though Travis and I were downstairs watching TV, we could hear her all the way down there. We bounded up the stairs three at a time, and saw that Teresa and my father were already in Tiffany's bedroom. Teresa was sitting on the bed with her arm around Tiffany, comforting her. My dad was standing nearby in a comforting and helpful way. Tiffany was sobbing, hysterical.

"I haad p-p-put it right here on my dresser with all my other presents and now it's gone. I know it was there. It was. Oh, my God, that necklace was worth $500," Tiffany babbled on, sometimes in breathy gasps.

I thought to myself, yeah, Drama Queen. I wondered why Teresa would have let a sixth grader have such a valuable present in the first place.

Then, all of a sudden, Tiffany looked up and fixed her eyes on me. "HE TOOK IT," she screamed. "MARVIN TOOK IT. HE TOOK IT EARLIER TODAY WHEN HE WAS SNOOPING IN HERE."

Was it my imagination or did every pair of eyes in that room look at me – questioning, accusing, inquiring? Did I even recognize my dad's eyes as he joined the others in a stare that made me look down in shame, like I was guilty of a crime?

But it was a crime I hadn't committed. So why did I feel so guilty?

Chapter 14
Falsely Accused

The next day was pretty much like the day before, with some major exceptions. My dad and Teresa had both gone to work, but Teresa had said the night before that she would have to call her homeowners' insurance today and put a claim in on the "stolen," (but then she corrected herself) "missing" 14K gold chain. My dad had come into my "loft" the night before and asked me if I had taken Tiffany's chain. He said it didn't really matter if I had, that he would forgive me, but it was important to return it if I had taken it. I told him I hadn't taken the chain, and asked him why didn't anyone believe me? Why didn't anyone accuse Travis or someone else? Why was I always the one who got in trouble?

He assured me that I wasn't in "trouble," unless of course I was lying. I had assured him that I hadn't stolen anything, especially NOT Tiffany's chain. I hated Tiffany for making my dad doubt me, his own son.

So I decided to do a little investigating on my own to clear my good name. I figured clumsy Tiffany had dropped her chain behind the dresser or something. So about 4 p.m., I snuck into Tiffany's room while she was watching TV downstairs. I pulled her dresser away from the wall and reached my hand behind the dresser, creeping it along the carpet. My heart was beating so fast; I just hoped no one popped in on me. They'd never understand and I'd feel like a real criminal. I could see something shiny! It could be the necklace, but I couldn't reach it with my hand.

I looked in Tiffany's huge walk-in closet for a wire hanger. She had tons of those silky padded hangers and plastic hangers but no wire hangers. I searched in the back and found one that had been used for dry cleaning. With sweaty hands, I untwisted the wire hanger until I got a nice straight piece. It worked perfectly. I used it to scoop up the shiny object and pulled it out. There on the end of the hanger was Tiffany's gold chain.

I quickly pushed back the dresser and shoved the necklace in my pocket. I threw the hanger in the back of Tiffany's closet. My heart was beating so fast. I was happy I had found it, but what should I do now? I decided to wait until my dad and Teresa were home.

As usual, dad arrived "home" first, this time bringing a couple of loafs of French bread and some sliced beef in a carton to warm up.

"Kids, Italian beef sandwiches for dinner. Mmm. I'm starved," my dad said, cheerily.

It seemed like Teresa always got home from work after my dad had dinner prepared. As we all munched on crusty beef sandwiches, Teresa brought up the "missing" necklace. "I called the insurance company. Looks like it's going to be a major hassle to get the claim. I have to call the police and make a police report and submit the original receipts for the purchase and everything."

It seemed like as good a time as any, so I said, "I found the necklace."

My dad was the first to speak. "You found it, son? Where?"

"Well, I figured Tiffany probably dropped it behind her dresser, so I looked there and," I paused as I pulled the necklace out of my pocket and plopped in on the table, "I found it way in the back."

Everyone's reaction was totally opposite of what I had expected. I thought everyone would be so happy with me and would be relieved that the necklace had been found, but it wasn't like that.

"YOU HAD IT ALL THE TIME," Tiffany blurted out. "You didn't even go in my room today, you liar!"

"I did too," I said back, but my voice lacked conviction. I almost sounded like I *was* lying. "I even have proof. I had to use a wire hanger to reach all the way in the back. It's still in your closet."

"You were in Tiffany's closet?" Teresa said in a tone that made me feel like a serial murderer or something.

"I had to. I finally found a wire hanger in the back that was used for some dry cleaning or something. Come on, I'll show you."

I brought the group up to the room and role-played how I had pushed away the dresser, reached behind and then used the wire hanger to pull out the necklace.

But the weird thing was, no one believed me. They didn't really say it or anything, but I just knew by the feelings in that room, that no one believed me. Not even my dad.

The next morning, when dad left for work, I asked to go with him. I wanted him to drop me off at Markus' house, where I stayed for the rest of my winter vacation.

Chapter 15
January Blues

Did you know that people regularly suffer from depression in January? I discovered that on the internet while I stayed at Markus' house for the last seven days of our winter break. I felt so crummy after I had left Teresa's house. I mean, here it had seemed like we could be a normal family. Travis and I got along really great, and Taylor wasn't even that bad, especially since she was hardly ever there. But I could tell Teresa doesn't like me, like I'm this unclean being or something, not to be trusted in her spotless house. And I don't think I could ever live in the same house with Tiffany.

But the main thing was with my dad. As he was driving me to Markus' house the morning after I had shown them how I had found the necklace, he kept saying to me, "Now tell me the whole story Marvin, the WHOLE story about the necklace." I told him, "I have told you the WHOLE story, Dad. Believe what you want. If you don't even trust your own son, just forget it."

I looked up the word "depression" under my favorite search engine on the internet, "Dogpile." There was tons of stuff on depression, and I read a lot of the articles, especially on Holiday Blues and January Blues. It seems up north, where they actually have cold winters, many people suffer from depression in January. There's many reasons like the shorter days of sunlight and the fact that all the holiday bills come due in January. All I know is, right now, I truly feel that Life Sucks.

So I wasn't surprised when that's all I wrote in my journal in response to Mr. Martin's Journal Prompt: "What did you do over winter break? Write in specific details how you felt, what you experienced in sights, smells, sounds, all of your senses. Use challenging vocabulary words, and words that make the reader "see" and "experience" your writing."

I dated my entry, January 4. Then I wrote those two little words, "Life Sucks."

Man, it felt good to just write the way I used to write, brief and to the point. Why would I want anyone else to know what I "experienced" over my devastating winter break? Like I said, writing is a waste of time, blah, blah, blahing over a lot of stupid junk.

I looked around the classroom. It seemed everyone was writing like crazy. I didn't want Mr. Martin to come to my desk and see me not writing, so I flipped to a previous page of journal writing and faked him out. Instead, I thought about the remote chance of me and my dad ever being a family again. But why would Teresa ever give him up? After all, he took her kids wherever she wanted him to. He brought home dinner every night. He did chores around the house. He even pampered Teresa with expensive gifts, like the diamond tennis bracelet he bought her for Christmas.

"Oh, baby, I just love it," Teresa said, as she held her arm up in the arm with the bracelet hanging off her wrist, sparkling in the light.

The whole situation just made me sick.

Ms. Turner came to the door and Mr. Martin walked over to meet her. They talked just outside the classroom in the hallway. Mr. Martin had a look of concern on his face and kept shaking his head back and forth. Then, he went back to his desk. He sat quietly and bent his head down and folded his hands. Was he praying? Man, it looked just like he was praying or something!

"Okay, is everyone finished with their journal writing?"

I slammed my book shut, and quipped in a put-on ghetto accent, "Sure 'nuf. That junk be done. 'ight."

Mr. Martin glanced in my direction. Good. I was the center of attention once again.

The ol' Marvin was back. I had almost forgotten my rep that I had started school with that had always served me well – smart-aleck, come-back kid who makes everyone laugh with a reputation of doing the least amount of work possible to pass and get out of this sorry school.

"I'm afraid I have bad news," Mr. Martin began. "Since we're like a family here, I don't believe in hiding anything from you. Nicole has had a serious injury. She's in the hospital right now in the intensive care unit." He lowered his voice, "She may not make it. They're seeing if the swelling in her brain goes down."

Quinesha was the first to break the eerie silence that had fallen on the classroom. "What happened?"

Mr. Martin hesitated and then said, "She had injuries to her head, chest and back. Serious blows. The police are investigating, but they think that the blows were made by a baseball bat. In addition, apparently she had taken some sleeping pills that her mom had. She was near death when the paramedics arrived."

"Man, that stinks," Luis muttered.

"Probably that sicko-boyfriend of her mom beat her," Brittney said. "That what happened, Mr. Martin? He beat her and then she took them pills to end her life?"

"There's privacy issues here. The laws protect a person's privacy and Nicole is no different from anyone else. So the truth will come out and the people responsible for Nicole's injuries will be caught," Mr. Martin said. Then he added in a voice full of conviction, "Rest assured of THAT! Right now, all you can do is be a friend of Nicole. Keep her in your thoughts and prayers."

Man, I thought to myself. Life really does suck.

Chapter 16
Healing Words

"Hey Marvin. Please come up here. I want to talk to you," Mr. Martin said.

Dang, I thought. I knew that tone of voice. I was in some kind of trouble. Maybe I'd use a little of the ol' Marvin charm to defuse the situation.

"Yo, Mr. Martin. Wuz Up?" I mimicked the tone of the actor in *Scary Movie*. Mr. Martin didn't seem impressed. Maybe he hadn't seen *Scary Movie*.

"Marvin, I'm very concerned about this last essay you wrote. As you know, our big writing exam is less than five weeks away, and if you wrote this for that exam, I think you'd be lucky to get a 2, and that's failing."

"No big deal. I just didn't feel like writing that day."

"But it IS a big deal. That essay had no central theme, no hook, and tons of misspelled words. When did you start using slang and swear words in your essays? See here..."

Mr. Martin pointed to my essay where I had written, "The dress code sucks and me and my dogs want to wear cool _____ like baggy pants, big shirts and more cool _____" Well, you get the picture.

"And here in your journal, the first day back from winter break, you wrote –"

Mr. Martin was shuffling through my journal trying to find the right page.

"You don't have to look any further, Mr. Martin. I know what I wrote. 'Life sucks.' "

"Marvin, what's wrong? What happened over winter break?"

I became instantly self-conscious. I hate when people say, "What's wrong?" I automatically say, "Nothing."

"Nothing."

The bell rang, signaling sixth hour, where we D.O.P. kids go to our electives.

"I'll do better on the next essay, Mr. Martin. Promise."

"Marvin, wait. I'll write you a late pass for sixth hour. I want to talk to you."

Mr. Martin said goodbye to the kids like he always did, things like, "See you tomorrow, stay straight, don't get in trouble, be cool."

When the classroom was emptied, Mr. Martin pulled a chair up next to his and sat down in his chair. But instead of peering over me from his desk like the teacher, he turned his chair to the side, facing me, more like we were going to have this big confidential talk or something.

I started to feel hot and felt my throat close up. "Hey, Mr. Martin. Like I said, everything's cool. I was just being a wise guy, I guess. I won't do it again. I really need to get to P.E. today because we're picking teams −" I lied about the picking teams part but thought it sounded good. I started to get up out of the seat, but Mr. Martin motioned for me to sit back down again.

"Marvin, just sit down. Marvin, did I ever tell you about my childhood?"

"No, don't believe you did."

"Well, it wasn't the best, to put it mildly. My dad, well I never saw my dad much. Once in a while, he'd stop in our little house (if you could call it a house. It was more like a shanty.) We had so many kids in that house because my aunt lived with us, too. We kids all slept on a mattress on the floor. I think there was me, my two brothers, and a boy cousin who all slept on this tiny mattress. My mom tried to do her best – she cleaned for the hotel down the street, so we always had these little extras that a lot of other kids didn't have, like those little soaps, shampoos, and that kind of stuff. Sometimes we'd have leftover food from room service. A lot of those rich people would leave half of the food they ordered for room service, so mom would wrap it up in a sheet and bring it home to us kids. Boy, would we fight over it! Hands would be flying and grabbing and if you were lucky, you'd get something special like a piece of orange all fancy cut or little creamers from the coffee that tasted like pure heaven.

"My point is, Marvin, a lot of us have bad childhoods. You know what turned mine around?" He stared at me with his brown eyes. He had that way of looking at you that melted down all your defenses and made you feel like you could really trust him. I guess that's why he was such a good reporter.

"No sir."

"Words. I discovered just a few years younger than you are right now that words can hurt – or heal. I discovered that there is power in words."

"Oh, yeah, like you say, 'The power of the pen is mightier than the sword.' But to tell you the truth, I never did understand what that meant."

"It means, Marvin, that when you write, you empower yourself to influence people, to change things that are bad, to make wrong things right, to make people laugh, cry, and look into another person's soul. Writing frees you. Do you believe that?"

"Well, to one extent, yes. Because for a while there, I was really getting into writing. In fact, I really liked coming to school and was looking forward to being with my dad over winter break. But you know how those people at the magazine turned against you and told lies about you? Well, something like that happened to me at my dad's girlfriend's house."

Man, would my trap just shut up. I don't talk this much about myself to anyone, not even Markus. Even when I showed up at his house over winter break, I didn't tell him anything about Tiffany and the necklace and everything.

"Do you want to talk about it, Marvin?"

Would you believe that for the next 45 minutes I told Mr. Martin the whole story? I told him about big ugly Tiffany and how she calls me Mar-vin, with the accent on the first syllable, and how she says "How Special," in her sarcastic tone if you mention anything nice about your own life or something. I told him about how I felt like this vile person when she saw me in her room getting the video game. I told him how I felt like a nothing when my mom got me nothing for Christmas and how I felt like a nothing when my dad didn't believe me when I told him I didn't steal Tiffany's necklace. I even felt like crying, but I held it in because I was afraid that someone from our class would come in and see me looking like a big, fat wimp or something, and my reputation would be ruined forever. I told him how when I heard about Nicole being in the hospital because some jerk beat her with a baseball bat that I decided that life hurt too much.

"Marvin, I want you to turn all that negative stuff into a positive force in your life. I want you to take that hurt and pain and suffering and make it into a vision, a power that writing can give you.

"Marvin, I had great hopes for you. All the kids in this class are doing great, but I saw something in you

that made me believe that you could get a five or e
a six on your essay. I thought that maybe you'd even
choose a career in writing. Don't let the sick people of
this world ruin that for you, Marvin.

"A journal can be like a therapist. Write it all
down, write down all the pain and the guilt and the
betrayal and you know what?"

Mr. Martin had me mesmerized. I just shook my
head.

"It's gone. You're free. You're free to become who
you are supposed to become. Did you ever think of
writing to your dad? Writing him a letter telling how
you feel and everything. Well, I'll tell you what. You
write your dad a letter tonight and I'll turn this F on
your essay to an A. Then, after you write the letter,
you decide whether you want to just rip it up or send
it to him, okay? Is that a deal?"

"Okay, Mr. Martin. It's a deal. Can I go now? I
still have 15 minutes in P.E." I was anxious to go now.
After revealing so much of myself to another person,
I felt too open, too vulnerable.

I was anxious to get to P.E. But I couldn't help
thinking about my letter to dad. Ideas were flooding
my brain. There was so much I wanted to say. I could

feel my brain writing it for me right now, like on automatic pilot.

I never did make it to P.E. I ended up on the stairwell, pulling out a pen and a sheet of paper and scribbling in almost a shorthand because the words were coming faster than I could write them. I felt this indescribable feeling of being alive, being on fire, being filled with this energy. And I hoped this feeling would last forever.

Chapter 17
The Big Test

Dr. Thornton's voice resonated throughout the school. "Just one last word of encouragement to all of our eighth graders – good luck on today's writing test. I know your teachers have prepared you to do your very best, so now it's your chance to shine and be a superstar. I don't think I need to tell you that your scores on this important writing test will help determine our school's grade from the state, and we want to be a "B" school or better! So just relax, try hard and I just know you'll be successful.

"Don't forget, students, you earn dress down days depending on what score you receive: if you get a 3, you earn one dress down day; a score of 4 earns you two dress down days; a score of 5 earns you three dress down days; and a score of 6 earns you a week of dress down days and a trophy. Good luck!"

"Ooooh, I'm getting me a week of dress down days," Brittney cooed out loud. "I be looking sooo good in my hoochy-mama shorts I be wearnin'."

"Me, too, man," Luis said. "Whoever made up this dumb dress code anyway? I mean, hell-o? this is Florida, and it's hot here. Wearing these dumb long pants everyday gets so stupid. I mean, don't they know that these pants stick to your skin when you're taking the bus home?"

Danielle piped up, "I'm going to dye my hair purple and wear a short top to show off my belly button ring." Danielle untucked her collared shirt from her khaki pants to reveal her midriff. "See, I got it done over Christmas. Ain't it a beauty? Hurt like sh--, hurt a LOT when he put that piercing needle through my belly button."

All commotion broke out as we all got up out of our seats to take a good look at Danielle's belly button ring.

"EXCUSE ME," Mr. Martin's voice barreled out. "Did you all forget that we have a very important test to take in just a few minutes? SIT DOWN! Danielle, please keep your belly button ring under your shirt.

Now, most of you know Ms. Lockner. She will be our Proctor to help me administer the test."

Yeah, I thought to myself, Ms. Lockner with the big knockers – that's what everyone calls her. Ms. Lockner is about 40 years old and she has a huge chest, which she shows off in tight sweaters and low cut blouses. That's what gets me about the dress code – we students have to dress a certain way, but some of the teachers dress worse than us! It's nasty!

"Now, everyone should have their two sharpened #2 pencils and a test booklet. I need to read the following directions verbatim and then you have 45-minutes to write your essay," Mr. Martin continued.

I was psyched for the test. Ever since Mr. Martin had that talk with me and I had written my father that letter, I've been like this super-writer or something. After Mr. Martin had given me an A on my letter and told me that my letter was some of the greatest writing he had ever read, I decided to let him mail the letter to my dad for me. (I didn't have an envelope or a stamp.) I hadn't really heard anything back from my dad yet, but (this was the really cool part) just writing the letter helped me a whole lot. I guess there's just something therapeutic about writing –

like getting something off your chest or confession or something.

I looked around the classroom. Mr. Martin had taped newspapers over all our writing posters on transitions, vocabulary, mapping, etc. I guess that was part of the security measures for this test. Mr. Martin was still reading the test instructions when Ms. Lockner let out a loud shriek. She grabbed the front of her light pink sweater in the front, and I could see wings extending out the back of her sweater. Apparently, her bra had burst in the back and her enormous chest was about to explode out of her pale pink sweater.

It was such a hilarious sight that the whole class burst out in laughter. Mr. Martin tried to look dignified as he asked her what was the matter, but even he couldn't hide a huge smirk on his face. Mike yelled out, "Looks like Ms. Lockner's big knockers are loose!"

Roberto high-fived Mike and said, "Yeah, man, they're definitely off the chain!"

Ms. Lockner muttered something to Mr. Martin and rushed out of the classroom.

"All right, settle down," Mr. Martin said. "Time to get serious again. We're going to be the last eighth grade class to finish this test."

"I don't know if I can write now," Roberto said to Mr. Martin. "It's hard to get that vision of Ms. Lockner's knockers out of my brain."

"THAT'S ENOUGH," Mr. Martin roared. He read the last sentence of the test directions, "You have 45 minutes to write your essay. I will let you know when you have 10 minutes left. Are there any questions? You may open your test booklet. Begin."

Mr. Martin wrote on the chalkboard next to Starting time, 9:30 a.m. and next to End time, he wrote 10:15 a.m.

The classroom fell into an eerie silence. Everyone was busy reading over their prompt. Mr. Martin had explained that we would get either an expository prompt or a persuasive prompt. I read over my prompt:

Everyone has a favorite quote, saying or slogan that helps them live their life. It can be a famous quote, one that has been in your family, or even one that you have made up.

Before you begin writing, think about all the different quotes, sayings or slogans that you have heard in your life.

Now, write to EXPLAIN which quote, saying or slogan you would choose to be important in your life, and why.

Well, it was obvious that my prompt was an expository prompt because of the key word, "explain." I made my little planning boxes on my planning sheet just like Mr. Martin had taught us to. Now, which quote would I choose? What did they mean? A slogan like Nike's "Just Do It." Hey, that wasn't half bad. But what would my three reasons be? How about that saying, "One day at a Time." Nah, that sounds like that TV show on the re-run channel. Man, I'm losing big time here; it looks like everyone else is already writing! Bad time to get brain freeze, Marvin! I thought a little more, and then said to myself, "The power of the pen is mightier than the sword." That's it! That's the one I'll use. Now for a catchy hook to catch my reader's attention. I remembered back to Mr. Martin and the day he brought in the fishing pole. I can use a question, a startling fact, or a quote. I scribbled some fast ideas on my planning sheet and then put my sharpened #2 pencil to my test booklet and wrote:

If you had to go into a battle, would you take a sword or a pen? If you had to right a wrong, change attitudes, or influence people, would you take a mere writing instrument as your integral weapon? A wise teacher once taught me that "The Power of the Pen is Mightier Than the Sword," and I vehemently agree. That quote is important to me in my life because writing is a tremendous power that can motivate and influence like no other.

I re-read my first paragraph. Not bad. Mr. Martin had said to use as many big vocabulary words as you could. I already had integral, tremendous, and my favorite, vehemently. Man, it sounded good. I was on a roll. My pencil glided smoothly over the two sheets of lined test paper during the next several minutes, telling these judges who I would never meet, about how Nicole's writing in her journal got her mom's boyfriend arrested and put in jail. You see, after Nicole started to come around in the hospital, the police were looking for evidence that her mom's boyfriend had hit her before. They talked to our school principal and Mr. Martin. Mr. Martin showed them her journal from class. Apparently, shy quiet Nicole had told it all in her journal, about how her mother slapped her all the time and her mom's boyfriend had beat her several times and her mom did nothing to protect her. With her journal as evidence, the man was arrested and thrown in jail. Luckily, with lots of therapy, Nicole should make a full recovery. She's in her aunt's care now in New York. So, in Nicole's case, the pen (her journal) was more powerful than the sword (the baseball bat used on her head.)

My second example was how my letter to my dad changed my life. I couldn't believe how easy it was to write this essay once I got started. When Mr. Martin's voice announced, "10 more minutes," I had just finished writing:

The Declaration of Independence, The Constitution, and the thousands of volumes of words in the world's libraries prove that the power of the pen is mighty, powerful and everlasting, unlike a sword, which –like an old rusty razor blade – can rust, warp and become, ultimately, useless.

Yes! I had finally found the spot to put a simile! Granted, the comparison of a sword to a razor blade wasn't the best simile, but what did they expect from an eighth grader? At least I put a simile in it! In the last ten minutes before Mr. Martin said, "STOP. Put your pencils down and shut your test booklet," I just had enough time to re-read my essay and correct a few misspellings and grammar.

Maybe I was delusional, but I thought it was the best piece of writing I had ever written.

Mr. Martin buzzed the front office on the intercom. "Martin's class done," he said in an official tone. "Now, Ms. Lockner is supposed to be here to watch you guys while I hand deliver these tests, but she's not here. Do you think you can behave for 10 minutes while I take this into the testing center?"

"Mr. Martin, you know you can trust us," Quinesha said with a sweet smile, which was mimicked by most of the other kids in class.

Chapter 18
Prom Night

The next few weeks after our big writing test flew by. Our big reading and math tests were next and we prepped for those tests daily. Mr. Martin kept us pumped up by saying things like, "You guys are going to show whopping improvements in your reading and math scores! We'll be famous – maybe they'll interview us for the newspapers." We all just got caught up in his positive energy and electricity and believed it for ourselves. I have to admit, when we read aloud or did those practice questions in the reading test-prep books, all of us were doing remarkably well. Mr. Martin said we were going to make miracles, and we believed him!

The reading and math tests were long and they took up a whole week. Ms. Lockner was back as our class proctor. This time she was wearing a suit jacket over her blouse. I guess she wasn't taking any chances! Basically, she was there to ensure that we don't cheat or anything. Like who would I want to cheat off of? Roberto? No way! Mr. Martin brought in red grapes and peppermints for us to eat during our breaks. They're supposed to stimulate brain activity. You know, I think it did work, too, because my brain felt like it was a well-oiled machine during that whole week.

But the day after the tests were over, I went into download. That was it for me, as well as for most of the kids in school. Kids were bone-tired of hearing about the state tests, so more than the usual amount of pranks rose up around the school. Almost every day, there was a big event, like a fight in the halls, stink bombs going off, or a fire alarm pulled. Most of us thought it was great fun, but obviously the teachers and administrators didn't. That made it even more fun!

So we were really psyched for the eighth grade dance or "prom" as our school calls it. It was on Friday, April 7, from 7 to 10 p.m. at the luxurious Hilton Inn on the beautiful intercoastal waterway. Our principal is really great and goes all out to put on a super event.

Some of the kids say it's because she's so happy to see us leave the school and others say it's because about one-third of our eighth grade class will never make it to their senior class prom! Both could be true, but in some ways Dr. Thornton was all right; she actually might be putting on the world's greatest prom just to be nice.

Would you believe our whole class was going? Well, all except for Nicole, who was still with her aunt in New York. The weeks before prom, everyone just started matching up. Me, I ended up with Danielle, which wasn't too bad of a deal. She can be real nice when she wants to. My best buddy, Markus, went with Quinesha. We knew those two girls had something planned when they both came up to me and Markus before class and Danielle wiggled right up in front of me and said, "Who you taking to the Prom, Marvin?"

"I don't know. Haven't thought about it." (Like I said, I'm a man of few words.)

"And who *you* taking, Markus," Quinesha said, sashaying her hips from side to side, giving him this little seductive smile.

"Maybe you, pretty mama. What you got in mind?" Markus is always on the prowl.

"Well, we've been thinking that we should all go together."

"All right," I said.

"You guys renting a limo?" Danielle asked. (I knew she had an ulterior motive.)

"You want to go with me, or do you just want to go with us if we rent an expensive limo?" I asked her.

"Marvin, you know I've always liked you," Danielle cooed. "But a limo would be so nice. I just happen to have a business card with a limo rental's number on it."

She handed me a small business card. A picture of a white limo was pictured on it with the saying, "Helping create lasting memories."

"I already called the number. It's only $300 for the night. If we get 6 couples, it's only $50 a couple."

"Six couples? We'll be squashed like sardines. How many does it say it fits?" Markus asked.

"It says up to 10 people," Quinesha added. (I could see she was involved in this little plot.) "But if we bring Beljania and Brittney, they both be skinny. And they can each pay $25 because they ain't going with anyone."

"Like we are," Danielle added. "Right, Marvin?"

I knew women could be crafty, but I didn't realize that they started so young.

"Right," I mimicked her tone and voice.

"Right, Markus?" said Quinesha to Markus.

"Right, and what are we doing *after* the prom, pretty lady? I hear those limos are so dark, no one can see what's going on inside," Markus said directly to Quinesha.

"Nuthin'," Quinesha said, her tone changing. "And don't you be 'specting me to be making out with you or nuthin', cuz you just taking me, paying for the limo and having the privilege of dancin' with me."

She and Danielle huffed off.

Like I said, girls got their own ways. You guessed it – we rented the limo and all of us "misfits" from D.O.P. went in it – Marvin and Quinesha; me and Danielle; Jesus and his girlfriend, Benita; Spaz Ron (who almost didn't fit because he was wearing this huge white top hat to go with his tux!), Mike, Roberto, Luis, Beljania and Brittney. (Luckily, Brittney is very thin and she sat on Roberto's lap. He didn't seem to mind at all.)

Me, well, I just have to say that I looked tight, really fine in my black tux. And guess what? I had to get an extra large jacket and only size 34 pants. Who'd a guessed? "Bubble boy" Marvin was now a tight 5'8" tall and 175 pounds of muscle. Who would've thought a little working out and a change of diet could make such a difference?

Man, the way Danielle looked tonight, a guy could fall in love.

Chapter 19
Marvin's First Kiss

Could it be possible that Danielle was only 14? She looked like a totally different person – woman? – from what she looked like in Room 122.

I don't know a whole lot about what girls do to get themselves looking good (never had any sisters; neither does Markus). About all I know is what I've seen on TV programs like *Ricki Lake* or *Jenny Jones.* You know, when they do those makeovers and the girl is all raggy looking in the beginning and then she's like all hot in the end?

Well, Danielle, as well as all the other girls, looked just like they were on the *Ricki Lake* show. I heard the girls talking in the limo about which beauty salon did their hair and which salon did their nails and their makeup. They all left school at 11:30 a.m.. Doctor

113

Thornton had issued a rule that no one would be allowed at the dance if they didn't come to school (at least part of the day).

Like I said before, the way Danielle looked today, a guy could fall in love. She was wearing this long powder blue silky dress that clung to her, showing off her great bod. She must have been wearing some kind of push-up Wonder bra or something because she definitely looked good in that area, too, if you know what I mean. But the best part of the whole thing was her face. In school, Danielle always looked a little rough around the edges, occasional reddish pimples, bushy eyebrows, with her hair usually pulled up in a pony tail. Well, someone must have fixed her eyebrows, because they were all nice and clean and went up in this little arch at top. I guess it was the makeup, because her skin didn't have a flaw on it. It was the creamiest beige with hints of peach. Her eyes looked amazing. She had this blueish color on her lids and her eyelashes were out there. Her hair had been done (like most of the girls at our prom—they really go all out) at the salon and was in this half-up, half-down hairdo that had all these loose curls surrounding her face. Some of the curls had little fake flowers in them.

After the initial excitement of arriving – Ms. Turner videotaping all the couples getting out of the limo; everyone oohing and aahing about how cool everyone looked; teachers fawning over their students (but we didn't see Mr. Martin yet) – Danielle and I were dancing to this slow dance. I had my arm around her waist, and I couldn't believe how tiny she felt! We were holding hands and just sort of walking slowly in a box. (I had never really danced slow before.)

"Danielle," I started.

"Yes Marvin?"

"You look unbelievable tonight."

"Thank you. It's amazing what a salon can do, right?"

"Yeah, but it's not just the salon. They can't make someone ugly look good." I didn't know how this was coming out.

She looked at me, puzzled. "You calling me ugly, Marvin?"

"No, just the opposite. What I meant to say is that you couldn't look this beautiful tonight if you weren't already beautiful."

"Why, Marvin. You hittin' on me?"

"No, no, never mind."

"I'm joking, silly. I always knew you were nice. But I tell you what – you gotta be the best lookin' guy here. You lookin' so fine in that tux and all."

I was totally embarrassed. I didn't know what to say.

"I've been working out. You know, with weights –"

I stopped talking. I was in shock. Standing at the entrance to the dance area was Mr. Martin, dressed in this white tux. Next to him was this fine looking lady in a short black cocktail dress.

"Hey, there's Mr. Martin. Com'on," and I grabbed Danielle's hand and we went to greet him.

Markus had already beat us. "Martin, my man," Markus said, in his "rapper" tone, doing this hand greeting with Mr. Martin like he was his "dog" or something, instead of his teacher.

"Markus, my man," he echoed back. "Marvin, Danielle, Brittney, all of you look so good. You make me the proudest teacher here."

"You dressed up in a tux," Brittney said.

"Yeah, I had to dig it out of the back of my closet. Had it from my old days at the magazine."

Markus was sizing up Mr. Martin's date. "And who is this fine looking lady?"

Quinesha gave Markus a quick elbow to his side.

"Hey, that hurt," he said, rubbing his side.

"This is Tamara Golden."

Suddenly, the music of "YMCA" blared out and the girls all cooed at the same time, putting their hands up in the shape of a Y.

Brittney grabbed Roberto's hand and started the move to the dance floor. We all followed, even Mr. Martin and Tamara.

We had a blast. Not only did we dance to the song, "YMCA," but we also fast danced, slow danced, did a Congo line, did the Macarana, and even a few country line dances.

"I have to go to the rest room," Danielle said.

"I'll go with you," I said. I needed a break.

We walked past all the fancy trays that were lined with chocolate-frosted brownies, fresh fruit and an array of soft drinks and bottled water. Danielle grabbed some grapes and a bottled water, so I did too.

We had to walk past all the teacher chaperones and even the police they had hired for the event. The restroom was down the hall, which was lined with all these palm trees in terra-cotta pots. There was a line at the girls' bathroom.

"Oh, man, look at that line. Let's go sit over there and wait until it goes down," Danielle said.

She was pointing to this little bench against the wall next to this lit-up fountain. We both sat down.

"Isn't this great?" Danielle said, popping a grape in her mouth.

"Yeah, I never danced so much in my life." I opened my bottle of water and took a long slug.

"Looks like the line is going down," Danielle said, as she started to get up.

"No, let's just chill for a few minutes, okay?" I said, as I reached for Danielle. She kinda fell on me and I caught her. She did this little chuckle and straightened her dress and then sat back down.

She twirled some of those curls on the side of her face. "I don't have to go that bad," she said. "Here, have a grape," and she popped a grape in my mouth.

There was something about the way she did that, something about the way she had fallen in my arms, something about the way we danced together, that made me do something I had never done before.

My arm magically lifted itself from my body, like it had a mind of its own. It went around her back and pulled her toward me. She looked down and then she looked up at me and started to bring her face toward me. I was moving toward her and then I started to think, "What if I mess up? What if she laughs at me?"

The kiss lasted for – I don't really know. I had this feeling like my brain was filled with clouds or cotton balls or something. It was nice, really nice. Danielle smelled so good and the whole thing was, well, pretty cool.

"Marvin, where'd you learn to kiss like that?" Danielle asked.

I'd never tell her that that was my first kiss. Someone once said that to answer a question that you don't want to answer, just ask another question.

"Where did you learn to kiss like that?" I asked.

She just laughed and kinda hit me with her hand, letting it rest on my chest a moment.

"Oh, the line to the rest room is down. We'd better go, there's only about 15 minutes left."

In 15 minutes, we'd all be piling back in our limo. I wondered if I'd get the chance to kiss Danielle again. Nah, it'd be pretty hard with 10 other kids in the limo. Unless we had the driver drop off everyone else first and we went home last?!

"Danielle, let's dump off everyone first and be the last two people in the limo. What do you think?"

"Marvin, that would be so cool. It would be like it was our own limo."

Instead of dancing the last 15 minutes, I made up this map of directions for the driver. First to go was Ron, Roberto and Luis. They lived in the same general area. Then, Beljania and Brittney, just a few blocks away. Next were Mike, Jesus and Benita and Quinesha. That would leave just me, Markus and Danielle. Since Markus and I were both going back to his home, Danielle would be dropped off just before us.

"Hey, Markus, I got it set that we drop off everyone before us, so we get to enjoy the limo the most since we were the ones who set it up, right?"

"Right," Markus said. "Am I going to get any alone time with Quinesha?"

"Well, she needs to get off with Mike, Jesus and Benita," I answered, knowing that he wouldn't like the answer.

"Man, I have all the luck," he said.

"Hey, Markus, we got about five minutes between stops before we drop off Danielle just before your house. You think you could look out the window or something just in case if I want a little privacy?"

"You mean with those dark tinted windows? What am I going to be looking at?"

"I don't know, just fake it. I just wanted to see if I couldn't, you know, get another chance to kiss Danielle."

"What'd you mean, *another* chance? You mean, you already been making out?"

"Not making out. Not like that. Hey, never mind. It's all worked out. Just examine the tints, all right?"

To sum up the night, my map worked out great. Between "Goodbyes" and "I'll call you tomorrow," everyone filtered out. I couldn't help but notice that Markus and Quinesha seemed rather cozy themselves.

My good buddy, Markus, didn't let me down. When it was just the three of us, he was looking out the window so intently, it was just like it was just me and Danielle.

"Marvin, I had sooo much fun tonight, didn't you?" Danielle said. "It's just like that little card on the limo rental said, 'Creating lasting memories.' "

I couldn't have agreed more.

Chapter 20
An Unexpected Visitor

Remember how I told you my life is like a roller coaster? When I'm up, I'm really up. But then it seems like something always makes my life come crashing down. Well, after prom I was in this really great mood. Think about it – there's only two more months of school left and then a long summer vacation. (We get off in South Florida right after Memorial Day weekend.) The whole prom thing was pretty remarkable and I kept going over it in my mind, which kept me in a great mood.

So I really didn't know what to expect when I saw my dad standing just outside my classroom on a Friday afternoon as I headed out to the buses with Markus. I was going home with him (as usual).

"Hey, Marvin," my dad called out. "Hey, Markus, how's it going?" He did this hand-jive thing with Markus, like they were rapper pals or something. My dad is pretty cool.

He looked a little more worn out than usual. I guess he was getting old. But he still had a pretty impressive presence – about 5'11", athletic, brown hair. In my mind, I'll always see him as I did when he was my football coach years ago.

"Marvin, I need to talk to you. How about I take you out to dinner?"

Oh, no, I thought to myself. What was this all about? "Sure," I answered. "Can Markus come, too?"

"Another time, for sure. But today, we've got some – you know, father and son stuff to go over," he answered.

Markus said, "Sure, no problem. See you later – or whatever – Marvin."

My mind was like on overdrive. It raced through possible reasons for my dad to come to my school. Was he getting married? Did something happen to my mom? Did it have anything to do with the letter I had written him? Did he even get the letter?

We basically made small talk on the way to Denny's. He talked about his job and I talked about school and the prom. At Denny's I ordered the cheeseburger platter and dad ordered some steak stir-fry thing. I was dipping a French fry into a mound of ketchup when my dad said to me, "I got your letter, Marvin."

"Mmhmmm," was all I managed to say.

"I'm glad you wrote to me, Marvin. It really made me think about what I was doing with my life. I mean, here I was bringing food home every day for Teresa's kids and I didn't even know what you were eating."

"Oh, Markus's mom buys some pretty good stuff," I said. "We like macaroni and cheese, spaghetti and meatballs, ravioli, that kind of stuff."

"Looks like you've been putting on some muscle."

"I've been working out with some weights Mr. Martin gave me. I've totally changed my lunch at school. This is the first French fry I've eaten in months. I usually get the sub sandwich, a salad and a banana. I even switched from chocolate milk to 1% milk."

"It's definitely paid off. You might want to try out for football your freshman year. Speaking of football, remember how close we were when I was your coach?"

I just nodded. Remembering how it used to be and how it was now was just too painful.

"I don't know how it happened, Marvin. I guess when your mom left me and Teresa started to show me some attention, I couldn't believe she could be interested in a plain ol' guy like me. I'm sorry I let my own emotions and my own problems hurt you."

"Ah, forget it," I offered.

"No, now listen to me, Marvin. These are things I need to say to you. I'm sorry about how you were falsely accused of stealing Tiffany's necklace. I'm glad you wrote to me about how it made you feel. You know, after you left, Tiffany must have lost that necklace at least 4 more times. I don't know why Teresa spent so much money on a present like that for an 11 year old!"

"Exactly what I thought," I agreed. It was a nice feeling of being here with my dad. We were bonding again after a long time apart.

"Your mom had the baby," dad said.

"She did? What was it, a boy or a girl?"

"It was a girl. You have a sister, Marvin."

"That's cool. As long as she's nothing like Tiffany," I said with a laugh.

Dad laughed with me.

So that was why he took me out to dinner, to tell me that mom had her baby.

The waitress came to clear away our plates. "Check, sir?"

"Yeah, sure," my dad answered.

I was getting up out of my seat to leave, but my dad said, "Sit down Marvin. I have to tell you something."

What else, I thought to myself.

"I broke up with Teresa."

"You didn't have to do that for me, dad."

"I didn't do it for you, Marvin. Well, partly maybe. But I did it for me. I started feeling like I was an unpaid nanny or something. It got to the point that Teresa was writing down for me all the different places she wanted me to drive her kids to after school. Travis got a part-time job at Winn Dixie, so she had me driving him to and from work. Meanwhile, *she* was getting her nails done, or working out at the gym. The final straw was when "big Ray" called the house asking for Teresa.

"Who's 'big Ray'?" I asked.

"Apparently he's a body-builder from the gym that Teresa had been working out with. When I confronted her about 'big Ray,' she told me he was just an acquaintance. So I did a little investigating on my own. I parked outside the gym when she was

127

supposed to be leaving and I saw her and this big young guy walking out with their arms around each other. That was it for me."

"Sorry for you, dad," I said.

"Hey, did you keep your menu? Do you want to order dessert, son?"

I couldn't remember the last time my dad called me 'son.'

"I pretty much skip desserts now, dad. Unless you insist."

"I insist. We need to celebrate. You know, Marvin, moving out of Teresa's home was the best thing I ever did. I got us a great apartment not far from here. It's a two-bedroom, so you've got your own room, Marvin."

My own room. It had been months and months since I had my own room.

"Man, now that I'm not driving Teresa's kids around every day, I feel like a free man. I've got more time on my hands than I know what to do with! Hey, remember that old football field at Johnston High School? How about you and I going over there and throwing the ol' football around?"

"Maybe tomorrow, dad. I don't think I'll be in the mood after I eat this fudge brownie dessert that I'm going to order. Tonight, I just want to see my own bedroom."

Like I said, my life is like a roller coaster, and right now, I was soaring to the top of the ride. It was a feeling I never wanted to let go of. The power of the pen. I was a believer.

Chapter 21
Feeling Like Winners

Did you ever read *Alice in Wonderland* or see the movie? Remember the Cheshire cat who had a huge grin from ear to ear? Well, that's what Mr. Martin looked like when we came into class on May 1. He was also bouncing around like a kid waiting for a birthday party or a holiday. Something was definitely up. Our class was decorated with streamers and two boxes of Krispy Kreme donuts were on this little student desk in front of Mr. Martin's big teacher desk. (In case you never ate a Krispy Kreme donut, let me tell you about these wonderful donuts. I think they make them mostly in the south, like here in Florida. They are so good, especially when they're warm, which it sure seemed like they were, because a wonderful aroma was permeating our classroom.) It was too much for Quinesha, who was groaning with delight. "MMMMmmmm, I just loove Krispy Kreme donuts, Mr. Martin. What are we celebrating?"

"Sit down everyone. I have important news for you. We are celebrating the highest writing scores (on the average) for any 8th grade language arts class in this building!"

Wild hoots and hollers rang out in the classroom. Mike and Roberto jumped out of their seats and were play-punching each other. Brittney was saying, "We bad, we bad, watch out, 'cause we bad." (In case you're new to middle schoolers and the way they talk, in Brittney's case "bad" means "cool," "super," etc.)

"How'd we do on math and reading, Mr. Martin?" Ron asked.

"The state won't have those results until the end of May. They have to grade all of those short response answers, so it takes a longer time. Our writing scores were unbelievable. We even had one score of 6."

"A six?" Jesus asked, in astonishment.

"Who was it? Was it me, Mr. Martin?" Quinesha practically screamed.

"No, Quinesha, you got a – " Mr. Martin scanned an official looking report he was holding. "Now let me check. Here it is – a '5.'"

She let out a high pitched scream, "I got a 5, I got a 5!"

Roberto was holding his hands over his ears. "Hey, you're going to burst my ear drums."

A chorus of voices blurted out at the same time, "What'd I get? Mr. Martin, what'd I get?"

"Settle down, settle down," Mr. Martin said, but you could tell he was so happy he was just like a kid in a candy store. "I have to show you your score in private, because of privacy laws. So one by one, you can come up, and I'll tell you your score. I just want to tell you that our average was 4.6, way higher than any other class. In fact, that score is way above the state average of 3.6 and the school average of 3.8. I am so proud of you. You guys did it! You are winners."

"Who got the 6? Who got the 6?" Brittney asked.

Mr. Martin paused for effect. "Marvin McDonald got the 6, the only 6 in our entire school."

Everyone looked at me in astonishment. I guess it was a shock for them, just like it was for me, to think I got the highest writing score in the whole school. What would that do to my rep for being the kid who did the least amount of work to just pass and get out of middle school? Suddenly, I couldn't give a rat's behind about my "rep." I was a writer, and I was a good – no, make that excellent – I was the best writer in the whole school, and that was way more cool than anything else.

"We also had a score of 5.5, which means that one of the judges thought the essay was a 6 and one thought the essay was a 5, so that is a very remarkable score. That belongs to Danielle," Mr. Martin said.

Danielle had a huge smile on her face. It was too much for the rest of our class. "What'd I get? What'd I get?" they all shouted out at Mr. Martin.

"Now, now, settle down. Here, come up for a donut and some orange juice, and I'll call your names alphabetically so you can see your score."

Even though Mr. Martin told each person their score individually, nothing was secret in our class. Inevitably, after someone got their score, they either blurted it out, like Jesus who screamed, "I got a 4.5. Oh, yeah, I got a 4.5," or someone asked something like Luis did to Roberto, "Dog, what'd you get?" and everyone heard the answer. So, all in all, I knew the scores of everyone in class. It went like this, highest to lowest: Me, 6; Danielle, 5.5; Markus and Quinesha, 5; Mike, Jesus, Beljania and Brittney all got 4.5; while Ron, Roberto, and Luis all got 4. Nobody in our class got a 3, which is considered barely passing. It was like a miracle. But any of us in Mr. Martin's class knew it was because Mr. Martin had believed in us first and then made us believe in ourselves. It was because of all the vocabulary we learned, all the writing techniques like "hooks" and similes and stuff. It was because of all of the sample writing exams we took, even though we hated taking them week after week.

Amid all the frivolity and excitement, I couldn't help but think that if it wasn't for Mr. Martin, I probably would have gotten a 3. No other teacher would have cared enough about us to really give a hoot. I bet our average with any other teacher would have been like a 3.

"Hey, let's hear it for Mr. Martin, who turned a bunch of D.O.P. kids into super writers," I shouted out above the noise. Everyone joined in and said things like, "You're the man, Mr. Martin," "Thanks, Mr. Martin," "You're my dog, Mr. Martin."

We almost didn't see her, Dr. Thornton, who had entered our room. She gave this big cough and said loudly, "Excuse me."

She didn't look happy or excited. "Mr. Martin, there's a matter I need to discuss with you privately. I believe the students are scheduled for computers now? Ms. Lockner will bring them to the computer lab, so we can talk."

We just noticed Ms. Lockner at the doorway. She gave us a weak smile that looked definitely fake.

Somehow, while playing "Where is Carmen Santiago?" on the computer, I couldn't shake the eerie feeling that something was wrong. Definitely wrong.

Chapter 22
Deceived

Like I said before, nothing is kept secret in our school. Middle schoolers love to talk and love to gossip, so here's how the story came down: Turns out, Mr. Kernel, who is our school's language arts department chair, couldn't believe that our class could have such good writing scores. Instead of being happy for us and proud of Mr. Martin, he immediately tried to find ways to invalidate our tests. You see, his test average was only 3.7 with his highest score being a 5.5. He felt that no way could some brand new teacher beat out his scores, since he had been teaching for 22 years.

Since Ms. Lockner (who incidentally is Mr. Kernel's girlfriend that Mrs. Kernel is not aware of) was supposed to be our proctor during the writing test, he immediately asked her if there were any irregularities in the test taking. For example, did Mr. Martin erase any mistakes on the way to turn in the essays, changing grammar or spelling errors, or even adding vocabulary?

Ms. Lockner told him that she wasn't there because of her bra bursting incident, so Mr. Martin could have easily done any of those things. I guess not having a proctor in the classroom during the test could possibly be grounds to have the tests invalidated. Since most of the faculty had heard about how Mr. Martin had quit his other job over "faking" that politician's quotes, they assumed he had done something like that to our tests. I guess they had all written us off as losers. In other words, they couldn't believe that we could be able to earn high test scores on our own. That really ticked me off.

On the way home to my new apartment, this kid – who I really didn't know – came up to me and said, "Hey, loser. No way did you get a 6 on the writing exam. I only got a 5, so there's no way you got a 6, you lying cheat." Other kids I didn't even know were pointing at me and Markus and saying stuff under their breath. I felt like a criminal, but I didn't know why. It got Markus real mad, and I had to talk him out of getting into a fight.

It got even more weird the next day. All of the streamers were down and there was this weird-looking old lady sitting in our classroom in the corner. She had a spiral notebook on the desk and a pen. She would look at us, look around the room, and scratch notes in the notebook. Mr. Martin looked nervous and instead of the exciting atmosphere in the classroom from yesterday, there was this tense feeling, like the saying, "You could cut the tension with a knife."

"Wuz up, Mr. Martin?" asked Luis.

You gotta give it to Mr. Martin. Even though he was obviously under some pressure, he came off as cool and professional. "Class, I'd like to introduce you to Ms. Needlebrook from our district's testing and evaluation department. She's going to visit our class over the next several days and she would like to ask you a few questions about your writing test. I'm sure you'll be glad to cooperate with Ms. Needlebrook."

"Looks like she's constipated," Roberto quipped to Mike, loud enough for us to hear. Ms. Needlebrook jerked her head back, like she was shocked by what she heard, and then she scribbled something down in her notebook. Mr. Martin shot Roberto this look that said, "Behave or else," and Roberto said, "What? I just said that she's contributing to our class. Contributing, get it?"

Mr. Martin continued, "She wants to talk to you individually, and she wants to begin with Marvin."

Hearing my name jolted me fully awake.

"Marvin, please sit next to Ms. Needlebrook and honestly answer any questions she asks you."

I hate to say it, but Ms. Needlebrook is definitely in need of some serious Botox injections. She had a big frown wrinkle between her eyebrows that made her look angry, even when she had this fake smile on her face. I made a mental note to myself to never go into testing and evaluation in my future career – definitely not good for your looks.

"Now, Marvin. You received a 6 on your writing exam. Do you know your I.Q.?"

"Not really. I'm not a genius, but I'm not dumb either. Somewhere in between."

"I see. Now, I'm looking through your journal and see on this date in January – just a few weeks before the test – that you really weren't into writing. I believe you wrote, 'Life sucks,' is that right?"

Now I was white-hot mad. She had no right to be going through my journal. That was personal. "Hey," I said, as I grabbed the journal out of her unsuspecting bony fingers. "That's my journal and it's privileged information."

Those bony fingers had a strength I didn't expect. She grabbed back my journal and, quick as lightning, popped it into this attaché briefcase.

"Now don't worry about that right now, Marvin. Do you remember using any big vocabulary words in your essay, Marvin?"

"Sure, I used 'vehemently.'"

" 'Vehemently'? How do you spell that?"

"V-E-H-E-T, wait, I can't spell out loud. Give me a piece of paper and I'll write it down," I said. This old lady with the bony fingers and the wrinkle between her eyebrows was getting on my nerves.

"What other big vocabulary words did you use?" she asked.

"I can't really remember. A lot. Probably some of them on that poster over there."

The lady put her glasses on and looked over at the poster that Mr. Martin had made that looked like a tombstone. All the "dead" words were in the tombstone like "good, pretty, nice," and big vibrant words were in the garden around it like "extraordinary, additionally, awesome," and more. She scratched some more on her pad.

"Did you look at that poster while you were taking the test, Marvin?"

I knew that it was against test rules to have any posters up as aides during the test. I also remembered that Mr. Martin had covered the posters with newspapers.

"No, Mr. Martin had covered the poster with newspapers. He had all the posters covered."

"Did you ask Mr. Martin how to spell any words during the test, Marvin? Did you, perhaps, say something like, 'Mr. Martin, what's another word for good?' during the test? Maybe you were stuck on how to begin, and Mr. Martin gave you a little help?"

Suddenly, I was filled with a resolve that I didn't know where it came from. The weak little Marvin always feeling guilty about something that he didn't even do was gone. My care and concern for Mr. Martin blanketed over any fears I had.

I said, in a resolute voice that had the ring of truth, "Let me tell you about my essay, and make sure you write all this down. I aced that essay because I wrote from my heart. It asked me about a saying that influenced my life and I wrote about how the power of the pen is greater than the sword. No, I didn't even know what that meant before I was fortunate enough to have Mr. Martin as my teacher this year. I wouldn't have even cared to know what it meant. And, yes, in January I felt down. Do you ever feel down, Ms. Needlebrook?"

She opened her mouth slightly, but I didn't give her a chance to answer.

"But do you know what? A teacher – that man over there who you are trying to discredit – cared enough about me, cared enough about all of us in this class that the rest of the world would just like to write off, to teach us to look within ourselves to like what we see. You see, even though to the rest of the world, we may look like a bunch of losers with below-grade level abilities, when someone really believes in you, you rise to their expectations.

"Mr. Martin is not just our teacher, he is our friend. And if you and Mr. Kernel try to do anything to our test scores – which we earned the hard and honest way – then get ready for a battle."

Ms. Needlebrook said in this weak voice, "Now, no one is trying – "

"Tell Mr. Kernel and his girlfriend, Ms. Lockner, to both learn how to teach. Maybe if Kernel really cared about his students, his writing scores would be as good as Mr. Martin's class. Maybe they should spend more time teaching instead of fooling around behind Mrs. Kernel's back."

"I believe this interview is complete," stuttered Ms. Needlebrook.

"It certainly is," I added. Someone once told me that whoever gets in the last word, wins the fight. "And I'll take this," I said, as my hand moved with rabbit speed into her briefcase to retrieve my journal. With my precious writings in my arm, I returned to my desk.

I had won; maybe now that bony old lady would leave us and Mr. Martin alone.

"Marvin, is everything okay? You look upset," Mr. Martin said to me.

"Yeah, it's cool. I just don't like them messin' with us," I said.

Instead of leaving, Ms. Needlebrook broke the silence of the room, "Next, Danielle Haywood, please."

You know how you get brain freeze sometimes when you drink something so cold? Well, I was so mad, so angry at the injustice of this situation, my brain felt like it had white-hot brain freeze. I couldn't think, couldn't hear the lesson Mr. Martin was teaching, all I could do was get more and more ticked off. I had to do something about this. But what?

Chapter 23
Losing Mr. Martin

You know how irritating it must be for a dog to have a tick in his fur? You can't get that tick out until you get a tweezer and pull it out. Well, Ms. Needlebrook was like a tick, irritating the "fur" of our class. She interviewed all of us, asking the same dumb questions. Some of the kids got intimidated by her and said stupid stuff or said they couldn't remember certain things. It made it seem like we were lying, or something.

At lunch, we were discussing it. Luis said, "Man, I hate that woman. She asks me, 'Did Mr. Martin take down his posters in the class?' and I say, 'No.' She writes that down. Now, how does that sound? It sounds like they were up for us to cheat on or something."

"Didn't you say that they were covered by newspapers?" I asked.

"Naw, that's what gets me. She never even asked me that, so I didn't say anything more. Man, I done Mr. Martin wrong."

"Don't blame yourself, Luis," Brittney added. "She asked me what a transition is. Now I know what a transition is – it's those little words we put at the beginning of the paragraphs. But I just went blank. I couldn't think properly. So I told her I didn't know. She wrote that down."

Danielle told the group, "She says to me, 'You got a 5.5 on your writing test. That means one of the judges gave you a 6 and one gave you a 5. That's an unbelievable score that very few students receive.' Instead of congratulating me, she then asks how I could write a 'perfect' essay, when my last year's reading scores were on a sixth grade level! I mean, the nerve of her!"

Quinesha asked her, "What'd you say?"

Danielle said, "I said that last year's teacher was a joke and he taught us nothing. I told her Mr. Martin was the best teacher I had ever had and he taught us everything about writing – about organization, focus, vocabulary, transitions, everything! And you know what?"

"What?" several of us asked in unison.

"She didn't write a word I said or anything. She just said, 'Thank you, that's all.' She then called for the next person. It's like a witch hunt, or something. They're out to get Mr. Martin, so she just writes down what she wants to write down."

When we returned to class, the "tick" was gone.

"Where's Ms. Needlebrook?" Jesus asked.

"She's gone," Mr. Martin said. A huge eruption of applause burst out.

"Is she ever coming back?" asked Roberto.

"She said that her report would be complete in 24 hours, and that I would get a copy of it," Mr. Martin answered. For the next 40 minutes or so, we all just vented about the injustice of it all – even Mr. Martin.

He said, "You'd think they'd be happy that you students made such improvements. Instead, they think we cheated or something. This is wrong, and it's an insult to me and to all of you. Hopefully, everything will be cleared up in the report and that will be the end of it."

But Mr. Martin was wrong. The report did not clear up anything and it definitely was not the end of anything; instead it was the beginning of a lot of bad stuff.

It all came down about three days after Ms. Needlebrook had made her report. Mr. Martin had not actually read us the report, but we could guess that it wasn't good because he kept reading it to himself over and over, muttering things under his breath, shaking his head from side to side.

"What does it say, Mr. Martin?" Quinesha had asked. He had just said that not to worry about it, that we should all be proud of our accomplishments.

So, like I said, it all came down – crashing down like the downside of a roller coaster – about three days after the report.

It was a Friday afternoon, and we were basically done for the day. Mr. Martin stood in front of his desk, facing us with a somber expression on his face.

"Hey, wuz up, Mr. Martin?" Luis said. "Looks like you're at a funeral or something."

No one laughed at Luis' little quip. The class quieted down. The silence was eerie.

"I have some news that may be upsetting to some of you, but I've always felt that honesty is the best policy and we are like a family here, right?" Mr. Martin began.

Several heads bobbed up and down in silent agreement.

"Dr. Thornton has decided to not rehire me for next year –"

Mr. Martin couldn't finish his sentence because all pandemonium broke out. There was a wild array of comments such as, "That's B.S. No way!" "I'll talk to Dr. Thornton myself," "Let me at that Ms. Needlebrook, let me at her." Several students popped up out of their seats, some with fists clenched. I myself was so furious at hearing those words, my breathing quickened and my brain got white hot with anger.

"Now, settle down, settle down. Let me continue. It seems that somehow things that I shared with this class in private about my previous writing job had reached Dr. Thornton's desk."

I felt my eyes avert downward, and then I looked around. Eyes were looking down; heads were hanging down. What had Mr. Martin said before, that it's not worth it if you can't trust people? Well, he had shared his personal story with us, and we had betrayed his trust.

"Well, I don't know who started to spread it around this school, but it had to start with this class, so that does hurt me." Mr. Martin glanced around the room. It was as quiet as a pin.

"The girls blurted it around," Roberto said, accusingly.

Brittney, Danielle and Quinesha jumped up and more pandemonium burst out. An array of comments like, "You crazy, we never said nothin'. You boys like to gossip more than us girls," and others were shouted out in the classroom.

"It doesn't really matter now, and I don't want you blaming each other. You all need to share a bit of the responsibility when gossip is involved. Incidentally, they got my story all wrong – they said I lied and cheated and none of that is true.

"So when Dr. Thornton got Ms. Needlebrook's report that said that she determined that there was no way that we would get such high writing scores, without some major test tampering, Dr. Thornton made the deduction – the wrong deduction I must add – that I have a habit of cheating or lying or some such thing."

It was more than I could take. I jumped out of my seat and words rushed out of my mouth, something about, "They're all wrong. You're an excellent teacher who doesn't deserve to be treated like this. We have to do something about this injustice."

The bell sounded and we all shuffled out to go to our sixth hour electives. A plethora of comments went out to Mr. Martin, such as, "Hang tight, 'ight?" "It'd be all right, Mr. Martin," "We love you," "Don't worry; it'll all work out," and others.

I walked out of that room, stunned. The injustice of it all burned me to my core. This wasn't just about Mr. Martin; it was about each and every one of us, too. They were basically telling us that we were losers and would always be losers. It was a battle between what was right and true and what was a lie. And I wasn't about to live with a lie.

Chapter 24
Marvin's Spotlight

Is it okay to deceive someone if the final result is for a good cause? You see, that was exactly the situation I was in right now. I had to deceive Ms. Turner in order to do something about the situation with Mr. Martin. It was a great plan, but would it work, or would it backfire on me?

Last week, I had told Ms. Turner that I wanted to start a new feature at her monthly PTA meeting, called "Writer's Spotlight." I told her that we could feature student writers, who would read their own poetry, short stories or essays. I explained that Markus and I could even build a little stage with spotlights on it and told her we could use Danielle's karaoke machine with the microphones. She said it was a super idea, and wanted to try it out at her last PTA meeting, May 15.

The only thing I didn't tell Ms. Turner was that I would be the only writer tonight for "Writer's Spotlight" and I wasn't reading no poetry! Tonight would be the test that would prove – or disprove – Mr. Martin's philosophy that the pen was mightier than the sword.

So far, everything was working out great. Our entire class was here and each student had at least one parent with them, including my dad, who was sitting in the third row. When I told my dad my plan, all he had said was, "I'll be there to support you. Just don't be too disappointed if it doesn't change anything for Mr. Martin."

It was a medium-sized group sitting in chairs set up in rows in our library: about forty parents, our principal, a dozen teachers, including Mr. Kernel, Ms. Lockner and Mr. Martin, who said he wouldn't miss me reading poetry aloud for nothing!

I felt bad lying to Mr. Martin and just hoped my plan worked.

Ms. Turner chaired the meeting, which she explained would be very brief because it was the last one for the year. After she ticked through all the mandatory items on the agenda, she said, "Tonight, we have a special treat. One of our students, Marvin McDonald, came up with a terrific idea to have a monthly 'Writer's Spotlight,' where students can have a forum to read aloud their original poetry, short stories or essays. I want to thank Marvin McDonald and Markus Thomas for building our artist's stage with spotlights and also thanks to Danielle Haywood for allowing us to use her karaoke machine. Without further delay, allow me to introduce Marvin McDonald, who will be reading us some of his poetry."

They say you can tell if an athlete has what it takes if they choke under pressure. Right now, I felt my throat muscles constrict so tightly, I doubted whether I could speak at all! Somehow, I made it up to the writer's stage and stood in front of the microphone we have set up on a pedestal. This was so bizarre; I had never spoken in front of a group of people before. What had I been thinking? I couldn't do this!

From somewhere, somehow, I had the courage to begin. "Tonight, I will be reading an essay entitled, 'Miracle at Monty Middle School.'

"How do you define 'Miracle'? The dictionary tells us that miracle means 'A wonderful happening that is beyond the known laws of nature.' A secondary meaning would be 'a remarkable example.' Did you know that we had a miracle here at Monty Middle School?"

I looked up from my essay and into the eyes of the people in the audience. "That, incidentally, is what we call a writer's 'hook,' which is defined as a catchy beginning to hook my reader's attention. You can use a definition, a question, a startling fact, a statistic, or a brief anecdote. Our teacher, Mr. Martin, taught us about hooks."

Ms. Turner, who had had a big smile on her face, looked serious now. A few people shifted in their seats. It was too late for me to turn back now.

I continued, "To begin with, our Miracle at Monty Middle School was a wonderful happening. It all began on the first day of school, September 7, in Room 122. Inside that classroom were 12 of the most whacked-out misfit kids any teacher would NOT want to have to teach all day long. Ms. Turner had been part of that miracle because she was with us until our new teacher was expected in. It seemed the teacher from last year had unexpectedly quit and Dr. Thornton had to search for a new one on a very short notice.

"Additionally, Dr. Thornton had been part of our 'Miracle' because the dictionary further defines miracle as 'beyond known laws of nature.' Certainly some divine force guided Dr. Thornton in her selection of Mr. Martin as our new teacher."

"Excuse me, but wasn't this supposed to be original *poetry*?" a voice rang out. I recognized it as that of Mr. Kernel. Dr. Thornton rushed up off her chair and headed toward me, "Marvin, I don't think –"

I turned and faced Mr. Kernel. I spoke directly to him, "In many ways, essay writing is far superior to poetry writing, at least the State of Florida thinks so, that's why we write essays instead of poems for the state tests."

I could hardly recognize myself. I, myself, was now acting 'beyond known laws of nature.' I guess the determination in which I answered Mr. Kernel quieted down Dr. Thornton, too, because she also sat down. A small smile of encouragement from Ms. Turner spurred me to continue.

"Mr. Martin was unlike any other teacher we had ever had. Before, our teachers didn't really seem to care about us as people. We pretty much did what we wanted, and that included playing cards, listening to our CDs, pencil wars and many other interesting–

yet quite uneducational – activities. All that changed with Mr. Martin. He had said to us that very first day, 'Who believes in miracles?' Most of us wouldn't have known a miracle if it was looking at us in the face. All of us came from different backgrounds with many different challenges – but no miracles. But that didn't stop Mr. Martin, who told us that we would be working on some miracles this year. He was going to create miracles for Dr. Penny Thornton, who was striving this year to get a good school grade from the State of Florida. But he wasn't going to just create miracles for our principal, or our state. He was going to create miracles for us.

"That first day, he told us that we were important. I didn't believe it. I was used to being the kid who other kids teased because I was fat. I didn't have much self-esteem and was going through a lot of stuff at home, too. But, through time, I came to believe in that miracle and came to believe in myself, also.

"Furthermore – incidentally, those words that begin my body paragraphs are called 'transitions.' Words like additionally, furthermore and moreover are transitions and you must use them to get a high score on the 8th grade writing state exams. Mr. Martin taught us all about transitions and how they connect ideas. Did I mention to you that I got the highest score on my test – a '6.'" A few hands applauded, but others didn't. Many people in the room knew where I was going in what I was saying, and I'm sure a few of them weren't happy about it.

I continued, "Furthermore, the dictionary defines miracle as a remarkable example. Mr. Martin was a remarkable example of integrity, character and discipline. He gave us the tools to do our best on the state's writing, reading and math tests.

"Although we don't know our scores on reading and math yet, our writing scores were the best of all the language arts classes in the school."

A round of whistles, hoots and clapping erupted. Marvin, Danielle and all of our class were cheering, and their parents joined in.

I continued with a new determination to finish my message, "But even though we created a miracle, a tragedy happened that thwarted the joy such a miracle should have brought. It was like if a person looked at the miracle of a new spring flower opening for the first time and cursed it. It was like viewing the beauty of a morning sunrise while smoking a cigarette. Compare it to the beauty of a magestic mountain, ravaged by brush fires." I paused for effect and then looked directly at where Mr. Kernel sat. "Those are similes, which Mr. Martin taught us all about. If you use similes, you get a higher writing score." I paused and then continued.

"Our tragedy occurred when a few jealous teachers couldn't see the miracle and called it a lie. They couldn't see the wonder and the love and the faith and called it a mistake. Our tragedy occurred when a miraculous teacher was falsely accused and now will not be coming back to Monty Middle School next year."

A murmuring filled the library, but I continued a bit louder: "In conclusion, a miracle occurred here at Monty Middle School. And I, and my dad, and my fellow students in Mr. Martin's class, and their parents, embrace that miracle, celebrate that miracle and will do everything within our power to allow that miracle to occur again here next year.

As a favorite teacher of mine once told me, 'The power of the pen is mightier than the sword,' and the truth will set you free."

Students, parents, and teachers were all on their feet, clapping. Several of the parents had turned to Mr. Martin to shake his hand. Some of the girls were crying and hugging each other. I noticed Mr. Kernel and Ms. Lockner walk quickly to the library exit.

I walked to Mr. Martin and shook his hand. His eyes were moist and he was having some trouble speaking, but I made out his words to me, "That was an excellent essay, Marvin. A definite '6.' You proved once again the power of the pen."

Chapter 25
Last Week of School

So much has happened since that infamous PTA meeting that I don't know where to start. You're probably wondering what happened to Mr. Martin? Well, I guess my essay touched Dr. Thornton and made her realize that a mistake had been made. She asked Mr. Martin to come back next year and to even head up the Language Arts Department, but he told her that he had already accepted a position at the school district's Golden Coast middle school for kids serving time in a jail-like setting. I think Mr. Martin will be really great at that. I read somewhere that a lot of people in jail have really bad reading skills, so if Mr. Martin can help these kids now, maybe they won't end up in real jail when they're adults.

Did I tell you? Our reading and math scores for our class went way up; some of us jumped up two or three grade levels. This was the final vindication for Mr. Martin to prove that we did learn a lot, and didn't have to cheat. (You probably remember that Ms. Lockner had served as proctor during those tests, so we had an objective witness.)

Speaking of Ms. Lockner, now she's going out with our 7th grade assistant principal. Can you believe it? She and Mr. Kernel officially "broke up" when Mr. Kernel gave his notice that he would not be back next year. I guess he was so insulted when Dr. Thornton offered Mr. Martin the position of department chair, that he just quit!

As for me, life has never been better. After word got around the school how my plan helped out Mr. Martin, I became like a hero or something. We've been having this week-long end-of-the-year celebration because we got our official grade from the State of Florida – a "B." That's like a miracle itself! Dr. Thornton was so happy, she dyed her hair purple and the assistant principals all shaved their heads. During the eighth grade assembly, I even got a trophy for having the only "6" in the school on my writing test.

It's hard to see our little D.O.P. class break up to go on to high school. Some of us will be going to the same high school – Me, Markus, Danielle, Brittney and Quinesha—Sunrise High School. Roberto, Luis and Mike are going to Community Tech High School to specialize in auto computer mechanics. Through Mr. Martin's help, Spaz-Ron got admitted into the Choice School of the Arts. Now, Ron can spend real class time doing what he loves, drawing. As for Nicole, she's still in New York. Maybe we'll run into her again some day in the future.

My dad and I are going on a road trip this summer, just the two of us. We're driving up through Florida, Georgia, Tennessee and finally to Chicago. We'll visit my mom and I'll even get to see the new baby. It might be nice to have a sister – as long as she's nothing like Tiffany!

When I think of my last year, I know I'll never forget my eighth grade year. Even when I'm old – like 30 or 40 – I'll always remember everything about it, because I truly feel I was part of some type of miracle. And that is a way-cool feeling. The funny thing about miracles is that you can't plan them, you can't force them, and you can't just make them happen. But if you're lucky enough and perceptive enough to realize one when it's happening, you can join along for the ride of your life, a remarkable journey, and experience a joy and wonder like no other. And it doesn't matter how weak or small you are; I mean, look at me, Marvin McDonald. If an ordinary guy like me can be part of something truly great, so can you.

About the Author

Mary A. Monroe has helped hundreds of middle school and high school students learn to love the written word and enjoy reading. *Miracle at Monty Middle School* was inspired by her experiences with struggling readers as a National Board Certified reading and English teacher. Her goal was to write a book that culturally-diverse struggling readers – and readers of all ages – could relate to and vicariously become empowered to reach their dreams. She is a former freelance writer, specializing in positive attitude articles, and former public relations Assistant Vice President of a Florida Savings and Loan. She teaches ninth grade reading at a public high school and resides in Lake Worth, Florida, with her husband and three children.